DISCOVERED DISTRACTIONS

DISCOVERED DISTRACTIONS

THE DISCOVERED TRUTH SERIES ROMANTIC SUSPENSE
BOOK SEVEN

JULIE BAWDEN DAVIS

Roses ARE RED PUBLISHING

ISBN-13: 978-1-955265-12-6

ISBN-1-955265-12-7

Distributed by Roses Are Red Publishing

rosesareredpublishing.com

❀ Created with Vellum

ACKNOWLEDGMENTS

As they say, it takes a village. Here's my village. I'm supremely grateful to each of these fabulous people!

ARC Reading Gems
Julie Schlueter
Tara Bradley
Angela Barnes
Heather Wamboldt
Kery Bailey
Trish Darrenkamp
Marilyn Smith
Lisa Starkey
Carolyn Overcash
Susa Fraccaroli
Becky Brown
Rebecca Pruitt
Amber Mancebo

Pros
Sharon Whatley, editing
Judy Bullard, cover design
Kayla Curry, logo design
Kyle Kane, logo design
Sabrina Wildermuth, design consultation
Jeremy Davis, book design

ACKNOWLEDGEMENTS

To all who have made mistakes and transformed themselves to try once again.

Irena Martin opened her eyes to the glare of midday sun coming in from the hotel windows. Last night, she had flung the curtains wide so she could admire the Las Vegas city lights. Stretching, she reminded herself of the cat she had as a child. Flicking away the unpleasant memory of being forced to get rid of him, she ran her hand along the empty silk-covered pillowcase next to her.

Reaching to the nightstand, she grabbed her phone and read a text message from an hour before. *"Last night was wonderful, Danielle. Stay as long as you like in the room today. I'll see you tonight."*

"That isn't going to happen," she murmured, changing screens to check her bank balance. Her heart pattered to see the transfer she'd made last night after he'd fallen asleep. It came out of his overseas account, so he likely wouldn't notice until she was long gone. Pity, really. Irena rather liked him. He was sweet and kind and much better than most of them.

Feeling pleased with herself, she picked up the hotel phone and hit the room service button, ordering their most expensive bottle of champagne and a Cobb salad. That done, she went into the large bathroom and began filling the giant whirlpool bathtub, sprinkling in a generous amount of bubble bath and watching as the suds swelled and tiny bubbles burst. A loud rap on the door interrupted her fun. That was one of the things she loved about the penthouse suite. Requests for service were answered almost instantaneously. She peered through the peephole to see a bellhop balancing a tray. She pulled the door open and motioned for him to place her order on the bed.

"Thank you, miss," he said when she gave him an exorbitant tip. Why not spread the wealth? She shut the door behind him and took the champagne into the tub. Time to celebrate.

Gordon Bradshaw scanned the company spreadsheet on the hotel desk until he located the profit and loss statement. Way too much money going out and very little profit coming in. He flipped to the company's valuation and smiled. His assistant had done well finding this business. He'd make a hefty profit once he stripped the assets and resold it.

Standing up, he stretched his back. The ergonomic chair in his home office back in Aspen never made him this stiff, but he'd paid 5K for it. Reaching for his coffee, he picked it up and took a drink, grimacing. Another thing that tasted a whole lot better at home. Truth was he hated Vegas. The smell of desperation mixed with cigarette smoke made him gag. But he had an important meeting here tonight. A meeting that would get him one step closer to securing the funds he needed.

Irena got out of the bathtub and stumbled slightly, giggling to herself. She had vowed to only drink a glass of the champagne but had enjoyed three glasses instead. Time to get out of here. Most likely, he wouldn't figure out what had occurred until later tonight, but she never took chances. She had learned her lesson the hard way with that first mark years ago. And if she ever started to forget, the memory of him breaking her wrist reminded her.

After sliding on burgundy lipstick and applying black eyeliner, she took her long hair out of the pins and let it tumble down her back. After this score, she had enough to live the good life for at least three months. But she knew herself. Following a few days of resting, she'd get the itch to work again. She always did.

In the bedroom, she opened her bag and pulled out a brown cotton dress. She shook it out, grimacing at the wrinkles. No time to iron them out. Reaching down to the floor, she picked up the Vera Wang silver sequined dress she'd worn last night, carefully folding it and sliding it into a side pouch. Then she pulled out black flats and slid them on, glancing around the room for the stilt torture devices that made her feet howl. She found one shoe under the bed and another on the other side of the room. Grabbing her cellphone and charger, she headed out, turning to blow a kiss into the air before she shut the door.

Gordon made his way downstairs in the elevator, glancing at his cellphone as an older woman got in next to him. When the elevator door started to close, a woman's hand reached in. She wore a deep-green emerald ring on her middle finger. He watched as she snaked her way through the narrow spot between the doors. She must have felt him staring at her, because she looked up at him, her eyes browner than the wrinkled dress she wore. She flashed a half smile, then glanced away. Gordon had a couple of hours to kill before the meeting. He decided to follow her and see where she led him.

Irena knew the tall, good-looking corporate guy was following her, and it made her blood boil in a pleasant way. There was something about how he held himself that intrigued her. As she passed the gift shop, a diamond pendant necklace caught her eye. She decided to slip into the store for a moment. At the counter, a woman stood checking her phone.

"Excuse me, I'd like to see that pendant hanging in the window." She pointed.

The clerk looked up. "Of course." She went to pull it out of the case and brought it back to the register. Irena watched out of the corner of her eye as the man entered and went to look at sunglasses.

"Would you like to try it on?"

"I want it. How much?"

"Eight-hundred dollars."

Irena handed the clerk her debit card, resisting the urge to turn around and confront the mystery man while she waited.

The clerk frowned. "It's saying your card is declined. Do you have another one?"

"That's impossible," said Irena, checking her cellphone. "There's plenty of money in that account." She pressed a button and waited for her balance to come up, shocked to see it said zero.

"I had plenty of money in here an hour ago." Irena practically stuttered. "Forget the purchase."

Turning to head out of the shop, she nearly ran into the man who'd been following her.

"I'd say I could lend you a few dollars, but that's a little expensive." He nodded to the necklace as the clerk returned it to the display case.

Irena glanced at the expensive cut of his tailored clothing, and then looked in his face. He had gray-green eyes, and their intensity made her uncharacteristically uncomfortable.

"Thank you, but I'll live without another diamond necklace." She smiled, willing herself to not hyperventilate about her bank balance. "If you'll excuse me."

The man stepped out of her way.

Irena rushed toward the lobby. She'd get some air and figure out her next move. But then she spotted last night's mark coming through the front doors of the hotel heading her way. Spinning around, she scurried back into the gift shop and stood near the sunglasses, praying he hadn't seen her. When he walked by, she let out a breath. Theodore appeared to be in a good mood, so he probably hadn't discovered the money missing from his bank account yet.

Once she was sure he was gone, Irena hurried through the lobby and left the hotel. Out front, she raised her hand to flag a taxi, then stopped herself. She needed a clear destination first. She'd walk until she found a quiet spot to make a phone call about her account.

"If I can't buy you a diamond necklace, I can pay your cab fare," said a familiar voice behind her.

Irena swung around. Nerves on edge, she snapped before thinking. "If you work for Hector, tell him not to bother."

The man looked surprised. "I'm just heading out and thought I'd offer you a ride." He waved a cab over and whipped the back door open, getting in and shutting it. Irena watched as he said something to the driver, then the car headed out. When he didn't even glance back, she felt oddly affronted. Men didn't generally leave Irena standing without a ride. And penniless. Her phone buzzed. She dug it out of her bag, her stomach dropping when she read the text from an unknown caller. *I know what you did, and now I have your money.* Irena glanced around. Signaling a cab, she climbed in and shut the door, resisting the urge to lock it.

"Where to, lady?"

"What casino has the most peace and quiet?" she asked the driver, realizing it was an impossible request in Vegas.

"Caesar's Palace has a shopping area in the basement that's pretty quiet. You wanna go there?" He glanced at her in his rearview mirror.

She nodded, and he headed into traffic.

Who was Hector? Gordon wondered as the cab made its way to Caesar's Palace. He had a good friend at the NSA who could easily get some information on his mystery woman, but the chances of seeing her again where low, so there wasn't any point.

By the time he arrived at the casino, he had briefed himself sufficiently to know that he'd likely walk away from the meeting with at least three, if not four, new companies in his portfolio. Tomorrow, he'd be back in his house in Aspen overlooking the rugged, quiet terrain.

Irena could tell the taxi driver was pissed she'd given him a small tip. At least she'd tipped him, she thought, getting angrier by the moment at being broke. Her emergency fund was in an offshore account, but she didn't dare access it until she figured out who had cleaned her out. She had some cash on her, but she needed to preserve it.

Glancing around the lobby, she spotted a sign pointing to the mini mall. It indicated shops and restaurants—most likely fast food. The thought of going to a fast food place made her feel irritated, then depressed.

"Irena, follow my lead. And don't cry like last time. They need to understand what you're saying. You do a good job tonight, not only will you get a Happy Meal, we'll have a nice hotel room to sleep. I'll even let you watch TV and get as many snacks as you want from the vending machine."

Her father reached down into the flowerbed next to McDonalds and picked up some dirt, rubbing it into her favorite dress. He loosened one of her braids. Then she watched as he got into character, leaning heavily on the cane he'd gotten for the part. When he was ready, Irena trudged ahead of him, pushing open the glass door to the restaurant with her small, five-year-old arms, her father pretending to struggle behind her. When they walked into the restaurant, everyone turned to look at them. The crippled, struggling man and his daughter. Their main marks sat near the cash register, an older couple who had driven into the parking lot in a Mercedes.

"Go on, child," said her father in a weak voice unlike his robust one. "Get yourself a water and some French fries."

"Are you okay, Papa? Do you want me to help you?"

"No, child, I'll be fine." He stumbled then, and Irena ran to him. That caused the couple to both rise and rush to help.

"There, there," said the woman to her father. "Why don't you come sit with my husband. I'll help your daughter."

"That would be so kind of you," her father gushed, as he sat down gratefully. "Go with the nice lady," he told Irena, who proceeded to get a full meal for herself and her father, all paid for by the nice, unsuspecting couple.

3

Gordon walked through Caesar's Palace, the sound of slot machine trays clinking as they filled with coins. He couldn't help feeling unease when he passed men hunched over the blackjack tables with a dogged look in their eyes, shirt tails hanging out the back of their pants, eyes bloodshot from not sleeping for days. He'd pulled his father away from tables just like that too many times to count. His nerves ragged; the same words came from his father's mouth every time. "Just one more hand, and I'll win it all back."

Gordon shook his head to clear the memory. No point in dwelling on the past, he chided himself. It only led one way, and it wasn't up. This client was a gambler, too, so he often wanted to meet in Vegas. It was usually worth the trip, though. Gordon entered the restaurant and nodded when Ray waved him to a table.

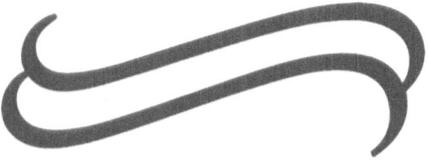

Irena found a spot in Caesar's Palace mall, where she bought a chicken salad and large bottle of water. The champagne buzz had worn off, leaving her with a sandpapery mouth. She sat down at a table against the wall, leaning back into the shadows. Her father had taught her to always blend into the background of wherever she was and give herself a good view of people coming and going.

First, she had to calm herself down. She stabbed at the chicken salad. Slow, methodical bites, she reminded herself. She then took a measured drink and set the bottle on the table. Who could have set her up and taken her funds? Not likely the last mark. She'd just seen Theodore, and he looked fine. More than likely, he was waiting for her to come back to the room and texting the burner she'd dumped in the hotel lobby trash.

No, it had to be someone she'd tangled with prior to this. Like Hector Pérez. She'd bilked him for thirty grand and took his pride and joy, his motorcycle. But she'd be surprised if Hector was here in Vegas. His playground was San Diego and Tijuana. Maybe he'd sent someone here to find her. Did he take her money to smoke her out, she wondered?

Irena eyed the various tourists milling about. A mother with a young child. A young couple sharing an ice cream. An older couple strolling and window shopping. No single men in sight. Irena sighed. She'd have to get dressed and make her way upstairs to the tables. She'd be going against all her own rules by staying here in Vegas, but she'd just have to bank on Theodore retreating to his home in Ohio and licking his wounds there. Another gambler looking for a good luck charm was her quickest ticket out of here.

When they finished their meeting and Gordon had agreed to buy all but one of the companies on the table, they ordered dinner.

"How long are you here for?" Ray asked, sliding a pudgy hand into the breadbasket and slathering a French roll with butter. In addition to a penchant for gambling, he had a love of rich food that Gordon noticed ended up around his middle.

"Just for the night."

Ray ordered prime rib and a loaded baked potato, then handed the waiter his menu. "I'm staying a couple of days."

Gordon turned his attention to the waiter and ordered a filet mignon, asparagus and a whiskey sour.

"I know you're not much of a gambler, but you're welcome to join me after dinner," Ray offered.

"I just might do that."

After an hour of shop talk and a filling meal, they headed for the blackjack tables. Normally, Gordon would have said no to the invitation to gamble, but Ray's business was significant, and he wanted to keep him happy. At least until the wire transfers were made.

They chose an unoccupied fifty-dollar minimum table and sat down. Gordon bought Ray one thousand dollars in chips and himself the same. The dealer slid their cash into a cash box and quickly counted out their chips, pushing them across the felt-topped table. Then he took out three new decks of cards and expertly shuffled and combined them. Stacking them in a big pile, he gave the cards to Ray for cutting, handing him a yellow plastic cut card to insert in the deck.

Gordon put out ten chips, then waited for his cards. When the dealer gave him a king and a three, Gordon tried to calculate the odds of getting another small card. The house's top card was an ace. When the dealer tapped in front of Gordon's hand, he nodded to receive another card, inwardly breathing a sigh of relief to see a four. He cut the air with his hand, indicating for the dealer to stop. Ray did even better with an eighteen hand, and the dealer broke, making the two of them winners for that round.

Irena slipped into her black, slinky dress in the bathroom. Then she put on her diamond pendant earrings and stiletto black heels and went to the main gambling hall. Scanning the room, she saw that many of the tables were full. She spied an opening at a twenty-dollar blackjack table next to an older gentleman. Generally, she'd go for a table with a higher minimum, but she needed quick cash to get out of town. This guy would do. Plastering on a seductive smile, she wiggled her way to the table.

"Okay if I sit here?"

The man barely glanced at her and mumbled, "It's a free country."

That wasn't promising. When the dealer gave her a dark look, as if to say, no taking space at the table without paying, she pulled out a wad of cash and bought a stack of chips.

As they played, she scooted closer and closer to the man, making sure to lean over and expose a little cleavage whenever she could. But he wasn't biting. She even flattered his gambling skills. Still no bites. After it became obvious that she wasn't getting anywhere, she resorted to counting cards. Irena knew she was taking a risk by doing so in Vegas. While counting cards wasn't technically illegal, casino management didn't like it. All she needed was a few grand, and she could get out of this Godforsaken city and figure out who had stolen her money. When the waitress asked what she wanted to drink, Irena ordered black coffee to sharpen her focus and got to work.

It only took an hour before Irena managed to make fifteen-hundred dollars above her original investment. She was just about to call it quits, when an iron hand gripped her shoulder.

4

"Come with me," said the man in a low voice. "You don't cause any problems; we can make this short and sweet."

He began to pull her away from her stack of chips, and Irena balked. "I am going to pick up those chips, and you are going to let me cash out, and then this will all go away," she said.

The man, who towered over her, kept his big hand steady on her shoulder as he pushed her chips back toward the dealer.

Irena shouted, "I want my chips! I've done nothing wrong." She struggled to shake herself free.

The man put his hand under her right arm and jerked her away from the table, leaning down to whisper in her ear, "You want to play it that way, lady? Let's call the Nevada PD. My bet is whoever you are, the cops are looking for you."

Guests were beginning to take note as Irena glanced around to see questioning eyes on her. A vision of the school playground, kids laughing at her, ran through her mind. No, no, no, no, she thought. She couldn't let that cloud her judgment. Stay cool, she urged herself.

"You're hurting my arm," she growled, struggling to loosen herself from the man's grip. "How about if I take the equivalent of what I started with in chips, and we call this even?"

"You're leaving." He turned and pulled her with him.

Irena had bet a big chunk of the cash she had tonight. She wasn't leaving without that money. If he was going to play hardball, so was she. "Help me," she cried, tears readily springing to her eyes. "I'm being forced into human trafficking. Please, someone help me!"

She heard a few gasps from nearby women, and several men stopped playing and looked their way.

The man glared down at her. "Really dumb move."

Irena continued to cry, the sobbing turning into wailing. Two other men with casino security shirts made their way across the hall. As her mind whirred, searching for her next move, she heard a voice say, "Please unhand her." It was the man from the elevator. "She'll leave peacefully," he said. "We don't want any trouble."

Irena felt the hand on her arm loosen. "You know this guy?"

"He's my cousin," Irena huffed.

"You both leave the casino now," said one of the security guards, "and that's the end of this."

The man from the elevator nodded, taking Irena gently by the arm and leading her away. After being handled by the brute, his hand felt reassuring and warm.

"Thank you," she said, when they got to the lobby. She pulled away, rubbing her arm. "They really should have let me get my chips. That's all the money I had."

"You don't have any credit cards?"

"They were stolen."

"You're having a hell of a night, aren't you?" The man smiled. "What's your name?"

"Kezia. Yours?"

"I'm Gordon. Kezia is an interesting name."

"It's gypsy," said Irena of her favorite alias. "Thank you, for in there." She gestured to the doors of the casino with her head. "I really appreciate it."

Gordon's smile lit up his handsome face. Irena realized as she gazed at him that she was having difficulty staying focused on the fact that she was now penniless with no viable plan. He looked at the large purse on her arm containing her belongings and then back into her eyes.

"Where are you going to sleep tonight?" he asked, surprising her.

"I have no idea," she said, for once being perfectly honest.

"I have a suite here, if you want to stay with me tonight and figure out what you're going to do tomorrow. I'll be checking out early to catch a flight."

Was he asking her to spend the night with him? Irena's intuition was generally finely tuned, but this hadn't been one of her best nights. Would she regret saying yes?

Gordon watched the woman as he spoke to her, mesmerized. She was gorgeous, with shiny black hair and intense brown eyes. But what intrigued him the most was her chameleon-like manner. Her expression and energy kept changing, making it hard to read her. He doubted her real name was Kezia, but it did appear that she was broke with nowhere to go. He rarely invited women to his room, but she intrigued him. He waited and watched as she ran through his proposition in her mind.

"That would be very nice," she finally replied. "Lead the way."

They went up to his room, and he swiped his key card, then pushed the door open, motioning for her to enter. He watched her glance around quickly. He'd have to watch his wallet.

"Put your bag wherever you want." Gordon went to the mini bar. "Would you like something to drink?"

"I would love whatever you're having." She sat in a chair by the table where Gordon had been working earlier and set her purse on the floor.

As he poured their drinks, he glanced out of the corner of his eye, making sure he'd put away all the paperwork from earlier.

Setting two scotches down on the table, he lowered himself into the chair facing her. As he held up his drink, Kezia smiled and tapped her glass against his.

"What shall we toast to?" she asked.

"New friends." Gordon took a long swig, then put his drink on the table. "Now tell me all about Kezia."

The children had surrounded her, some spitting at her feet in the dirt of the playground.

"Your father is a tramp," one child, a girl she thought was her friend, taunted her. "My mom says you're both white trash."

"Yeah, my dad says that your dad steals. That's why he's in jail." Another boy weighed in.

Irena felt a weight on her chest until she couldn't breathe. How she wanted to slip into a hole in the ground and disappear.

"Aren't you going to say anything?" demanded a boy named Charlie. He was fat like his father.

Irena remembered her father's words. Don't ever give in to a bully, or you'll be the bully's slave for life.

"You're a pudgy, little pig," Irena blurted, advancing toward Charlie. "And if you keep talking about my father, we're both going to come to your house and roast you like they do pigs."

That elicited sniggers from the crowd. Charlie's face reddened, and he cried, "I'm going to tell on you!"

Just then their teacher, Mrs. Baker, appeared. "What's going on here? Charlie?"

The boy pointed to Irena. "She called me a pig!"

Mrs. Baker scolded. "Irena, I thought we talked about this. No arguing on the playground. I'm going to have to speak to your father again."

"You can't," cried out one boy. "He's in jail!"

5

"The name Kezia means cassia tree in Hebrew. I come from a long line of Romani gypsies." Irena watched Gordon's face closely as she spoke. It was as if he was analyzing each of her words.

"I thought the Romani were mainly in Europe," said Gordon.

Irena took a sip of her scotch. "They were, are. My family came to the United States from southeastern Europe two generations ago. I come from the group of gypsies known as Kalderash."

"Where is your family now?"

"My parents passed years ago, and my brother is lost to me. So, I am alone." Irena waited to see how that last line would play out. Men often felt sorry for her when she said that and would go into savior mode. But Gordon remained expressionless. She squirmed in her chair and continued. "I say lost to me, because my brother decided to leave his roots behind and change his name. We haven't spoken in several years. But I must be boring you. Perhaps you'd like to talk of something else?"

Gordon was impressed. Kezia, or whatever her name was, had her story down cold. And all the triggers for sympathy. He had to admit he was having quite a good time with this.

"On the contrary," Gordon answered. "I find this all fascinating. I don't think I've ever met a real gypsy before. Tell me more about your origins. Where did you grow up?" He watched as Kezia ran her finger up and down on the condensation on her glass.

"We were nomads. I have never stayed in one place for long." She looked into his eyes, then past him to the far wall. Another sign of a masterful con, he thought. Mixing truth with fiction. She likely hadn't known a stable home.

"You seem to know your way around a card table. Have you spent much time in Vegas? Or is that another Romani gift?"

"A little of both. My father was quite good with the cards."

"Mine, too," murmured Gordon. "Which is why I generally stay away from the tables."

He watched as Kezia's spine straightened.

"I generally stay away, too," she said. "With my credit cards stolen, I found it necessary to play the cards. Do you have any cigarettes?"

Gordon shook his head. "I don't smoke."

"Your turn," said Kezia. "Tell me about Gordon. Is that your real name?"

He laughed. "And why wouldn't it be my real name?"

"You don't seem like a Gordon."

He leaned back in his chair and reached for his scotch. After draining the glass, he said, "Many of my friends call me by my middle name, Rex, but I prefer Gordon."

"I like Rex," said Kezia. "That's what I'll call you."

Gordon raised one eyebrow. "And now we're friends?"

Kezia laughed and leaned forward just enough for Gordon to get a good view of her cleavage, which gave him a warm rush.

How many times had she done that for strangers, he wondered? He stood up. "It's late. I'm going to call housekeeping for a cot. If you'd like to use the bathroom first, please go ahead."

He repressed a smile at the irritated flash that ran through Kezia's eyes as she stood and reached for her bag. "Thank you. I will take you up on that offer."

When he heard the bathroom door lock and the water start to run, he gathered his small valuables and paperwork and put it all in the safe. He'd have to sleep with his laptop under his pillow.

Kezia turned on the bathroom sink and checked the space for any personal effects. Gordon, Rex, whatever his name was, kept things tidy. Nothing in here but an empty hotel shampoo bottle. She was having a hell of a time reading this guy. And if his fastidiousness was any indication, it wasn't going to be easy to lift his wallet or laptop. He was a controlled drinker, from what she could tell. No loosening him up that way. She could only hope he talked in his sleep.

Irena decided to wash up and go get some sleep, on a cot of all things. The thought made her irritated and depressed at the same time.

"I have no idea where your wallet is." Irena's father had answered the banging on the door when Irena was in the bathroom. They'd been staying in a fleabag motel for the last month. Today was her turn to score some cash. Thirteen-year-old Irena had lifted this bozo's wallet in the hotel laundromat. He'd been dumb enough to set it in his laundry basket.

"It's not our problem you lost your wallet," Irena said, her heart racing at the rage morphing the man's face, turning his pasty complexion dark red.

"Give me my wallet back, you little thief, or I'll beat your father's face in."

Her father threw up his arms. "Whoa! No one needs to beat anyone. Irena, give him his wallet."

Irena watched the man descend on her father with his giant hands clenched. Would it make her father settle down and get the little house he had been promising for years if she let the man beat him? Right as he started to swing, she yelled, "I'll give it to you. Please don't hit him."

She went to the cot she'd been sleeping on and reached into her bedcovers for the wallet. It only had ten dollars in cash. The rest of his stuff was intact. She handed it to the man, who snatched it from her grasp and checked the contents.

"I oughta give your old man a black eye for not watching after you. Get out of here by morning, or you'll both be sorry."

When Irena came out of the bathroom, the cot was already set up in the corner. She noticed Gordon had put away his things. Was he on to her? She watched as he headed for the bathroom, his suitcase in tow. Maybe he was just being careful. She was a complete stranger.

After the bathroom door closed, Irena hurried to check the room. Drawers, closet, under the bed—nothing. No cellphone, no charger. Did he take his laptop into the bathroom with him? Irena was feeling more and more off her game by the moment. Just as she pulled up the bed's mattress, she heard her cellphone buzz. Heart in her throat, she retrieved her phone from her bag and unlocked the screen.

When I find you, I promise, you'll regret the day we met.

She felt someone behind her, and turned, a scream stuck in her throat. It was Gordon. Had Hector sent him, after all?

6

"How about you tell me what's really going on?" said Gordon. Kezia tried to back up, but her legs hit the side of the cot, and she ended up falling onto it.

"Tell Hector I'll return his money. I just need a little more time," she blurted.

"I told you, I know no Hector." He watched the fear in Kezia's eyes subside. "You owe him money? How much?" he asked, and she began sobbing. If they were real tears, Gordon couldn't tell for sure. He waited until the crying subsided. Then he sighed and pulled a chair next to her and sat down. "If someone is going to come crashing in here in the middle of the night, I need to know," he said.

Kezia mopped her eyes with the edge of her nightdress. "Hector is, was, my boyfriend. He beat me, and in order to escape, I had to steal some of his money. He's been following me ever since."

Gordon repressed the urge to laugh. This woman was a lot of things—obviously—but victim wasn't one of them. "Get some sleep," he said. Then he stood and got into bed, turning on his laptop so he could email his friend at the NSA with the photo of Irena he'd taken of her when she was unaware.

Irena lay in her cot as Gordon sat in bed tapping away on his laptop as if she wasn't even there. What was it with this guy? Were women not his thing? Or was he just stringing her along, waiting for Hector to come and get her? For a time, she contemplated waiting until he fell asleep, then leaving the hotel room. But she had nowhere to go. As the tapping of his computer continued, Irena eventually felt herself drifting off.

Just as Gordon was about to turn off his computer for the night, he got a return email from his buddy, Benson, at the NSA. He glanced over at Kezia, then clicked the email open. She had a string of aliases, and several arrests. Most for petty theft, and one for grand larceny. Only known relative, a father, whereabouts currently unknown.

Gordon sighed and slipped his laptop under his pillow. He'd figure out what to do about her in the morning.

When Gordon awoke, Kezia was in the bathroom. He glanced at the bedside clock. Seven a.m. His flight wasn't until noon, but he liked to get to the airport early. It would be better to part ways with her as soon as possible, before her trouble rubbed off. He got out of bed and went to the coffee machine, measuring in enough for two.

"Coffee." Kezia smiled as she emerged from the bathroom, looking freshly scrubbed and more alert than she'd been yesterday. "Is there a cup for me?"

"Yes. As I mentioned last night, I have a flight to catch. So, after breakfast..." Gordon trailed off.

"I'll get out of your hair, as they say," Kezia said. "Thank you for the cot." She gestured to the little bed, which she'd made up tidily.

He was about to ask her what she planned to do when they parted but thought better of it. If she said she had no idea where to go, he could find himself back where he started. He handed Kezia her coffee.

"Not too bad for hotel brew," she commented after pouring in two packets of sugar and taking a sip.

Gordon nodded as he drank his coffee, then set it down on the table. "I have a standing order for breakfast that should arrive soon. If you can get the door, that'd be great. I'm going to hop in the shower."

He headed into the bathroom and turned on the shower, the room soon steaming up. Unzipping his bag, he remembered his laptop under the pillow. He'd better get it before she made off with it. As he went to open the door, he heard a man's voice. Cracking the door open, he looked out to see someone holding Kezia in front of him. She was gasping for air in his grip. "Put the money back, and we'll call this even," he told her.

Gordon opened the door and in three long strides was behind the guy, wrenching his arms free of Kezia, who fell forward on the carpeting, hands around her neck, coughing.

The guy was shorter than Gordon and cowered as he held him by the arms in a vice grip.

"That's no way to treat a lady," Gordon heard himself saying.

"She's no lady. She just spent the last three days with me and completely cleaned me out. Better check your bank balance."

Gordon let go of the guy. "I'll see to it that she returns your money."

The guy looked from Kezia to Gordon and back again. "You two running the scam together?"

"He's not involved," said Kezia. "How did you find me?"

"After you disappeared, I came here to meet a friend last night and saw you getting into the elevator with him."

"Give me your number so I can contact you when I have the cash," said Gordon.

The guy shook his head and reached into his back pocket for his wallet, pulling out a business card and handing it to Gordon. "She doesn't pay me back within the next few days, I'm going to the cops." He eyed Gordon nervously as he backed out of the hotel room.

Gordon checked out the man's business card. "I assure you, Theodore, the police won't be necessary. We'll be in touch."

He shut the door and turned to Kezia, who stood with her hands on her hips. "I had that under control. No need for you to make a promise I can't keep."

"Who are you?" Gordon exploded. "Kezia? Gabriella? Yvonne? Danielle? Or maybe, Irena Martin?"

Shock covered Kezia's face. She began backing up, her eyes darting like a cornered animal. "I don't know what you want, but I don't have any money. I told you."

Gordon could almost see her brain working. She was one steely woman. One of the most interesting he'd come across in a long time. Damn, why did he always get involved with the wrong kind of woman? One that he felt certain would give him a run for his money. Still, she made his heart race. Maybe it was because she was so like him. Not that that was good, but he understood her, in a sense. She was scrappy and not afraid to take on the world, including anyone who got in the way of what she wanted. He got that. Actually, he admired it.

7

Irena's cellphone buzzed on the cot. Gordon grabbed it and checked the screen. He read the text message out loud, *"You think you can hide from me, but you're mistaken. I am coming for you."*

He looked Irena straight in the eye. "I'd say this isn't a practical joke. Who is this?"

Irena slapped both hands down on her thighs. "You know so much, you tell me."

"It appears that you've pissed off so many people that you haven't a clue as to who this could be. Am I right?"

Tears started to spring to Irena's eyes.

"Let's skip the waterworks."

Irena motioned to pick up her bag. "Fine. I'll just be off. Get out of your way, so you can get on your plane."

Gordon reached for her arm. When his hand touched her bare skin, he felt a welcome spark.

"Stop deflecting. Listen, I'm good at problem solving. I might be able to help you out of this."

"And why would you do that?"

Gordon saw doubt and disbelief in her eyes. He removed his hand from her arm and shrugged. "Because I can. And because you can help me."

Irena's eyebrows raised. "Go on."

"I have a highly lucrative deal that I need to close back in Colorado. It's an older couple. Very traditional. They think I'm married."

"You must have dozens of women dying to date you. Why not ask one of your girlfriends?" Irena retorted.

"Because all of the women dying to date me, as you put it, couldn't con a three-year-old."

Irena seemed to consider. "It does sound potentially amusing."

"I thought you might say so. But just so we're clear. This will be an even trade. I help you with your problem. You help me with my deal. You don't get a penny out of the transaction. I'm going to call the airline and book you a seat on my flight. Then we need to get out of here."

Irena kept an eye on Gordon as he called the airlines. She admired his drive and efficiency, as if chopping through a forest with a machete. She'd been on the road by herself for so long, she wasn't used to backup. It was refreshing.

Gordon hung up the phone and picked up his case. "Before we go, take out the towel you have in your bag. I don't want to pay extra just because your fingers are sticky."

Irena sighed and flung the fluffy white hand towel she'd stuffed into her purse onto the bed.

Irena watched the casinos slip by as they headed toward the airport in a taxi. She liked the action of Vegas. The smell of winning, and even losing, but she'd be glad to say goodbye to the last few days. The texts were really freaking her out. It could be Hector, but it really didn't seem like his style. Maybe she wasn't seeing something clearly. Irena hated being in the dark.

"Kezia, be a dear and buy your father a coke while I give this nice lady directions."

Irena and her father were standing outside of a Taco Bell in New Mexico. They were supposed to run a con inside for lunch, but this woman suddenly appeared. Six years old at the time, Irena could tell that her father knew the woman, even though he pretended not to.

"I don't have any change. Plus, we were going to get something to drink inside together." Irena motioned for his hand, but he reached into his pocket instead and took out a handful of coins. He poured them into her hand. "Get yourself whatever you want, too."

At first, Irena felt like she'd hit the jackpot, but then she realized what he was doing. Distracting her.

When Irena refused to budge, her father, exasperated, said, "I'll be right in. Now, Kezia."

"My name is Irena."

Her father blew air out of his mouth and looked at the woman as if to say, *you see what I put up with?*

"Fine. Irena. Now please, go get whatever you want with the money I just gave you. I'll be right in."

Irena reluctantly walked toward the restaurant, glancing back several times. The woman and her father talked in earnest now, and Irena couldn't hear a word. She went into the air-conditioned restaurant and bought herself and her father tacos and milkshakes, then headed to a window seat. As she slid into the booth, she peered out the window. Her father and the woman were gone.

8

By the time they arrived at McCarran International, Gordon was wondering what he'd gotten himself into. There was something about Vegas that made him act recklessly. Although, he had to admit he hadn't been this excited about anything in a long time.

They made it through airport security without mishap. When TSA checked Irena's purse, he realized he was holding his breath. After the agent returned it to her following a cursory inspection, he watched her clutch the bag to her breast, as if it was all she owned. Where was her home, he wondered? He realized he knew very little about her.

As they headed to the gate, Irena asked, "You have a home in Aspen?"

"Yes. Where do you call home?"

Irena hesitated. "The road is my home."

"You must have someplace where you keep all of your belongings."

"There is one place, but I haven't been there in months." She suddenly grabbed hold of his arm and stopped walking. "Those men over there."

He followed her gaze to see two men in jet black suits standing by their gate, eyes searching the crowd. When one man spotted them, he cried, "There he is!"

"They're coming our way." Gordon grabbed Irena's arm and spun them around. They rushed away from the gate into a crowd of people and out the other side. Spotting a busy restaurant up ahead, Gordon pointed to it. They slipped in quickly, locating a table at the back shielded by the bar.

Once they both caught their breaths, Irena said, "They said, there *he* is."

"I noticed that."

"You talk about me pissing people off. It's my turn to ask what you're hiding."

Gordon glanced toward the entrance to the restaurant, then looked at Irena. "It could be the SEC."

Irena began laughing. It started out as a chuckle, but she ended up doubling over and wiping tears from the corners of her eyes.

Gordon gave her a wry smile when she finished. "Point taken. Now we need to figure out how to get out of here. Where is the home you haven't been to in a while?"

"Prescott Valley."

"Arizona?"

"Dry and dusty, but it's off the grid."

"We're going to need a rental car. But they will want a credit card for deposit. I can't use any of mine until I figure out what the hell is going on."

"How much cash do you have?" she asked him.

Gordon thought for a moment. "Enough to get us to Arizona."

Irena rather liked how the tables seemed to have turned on Gordon. Not that she'd wish the SEC on him. She'd heard how nasty that could be to have your financial transactions scrutinized by the government. But she'd been getting tired of his superior attitude. Now that they were both on the run, this whole escapade would be much more enjoyable.

They waited a good thirty minutes, Gordon checking outside of the restaurant periodically to see if he spotted the men. She watched approvingly at how he dealt with the situation. Thoughtfully and with intent. Though they were sitting in a bar, he didn't get a drink to calm his nerves like many people would. Did anything ruffle him, she wondered?

Finally, they decided the coast was clear and made their way to the rental car kiosks. Irena scanned the employees behind each counter before approaching one.

"Hello, there," she said to a fresh-scrubbed young man who flashed them an easy smile.

"How can I help you?"

Irena leaned in close and said in a low voice. "This is so embarrassing, but we have a problem that we hope you can help us solve."

The young man's eyes widened. "I'll help in any way I can."

"We both got terribly drunk last night when we were gambling and lost our wallets, IDs, everything. We could call home, but our families won't help us. They're tired of our gambling problem."

"I'm not sure how I can help."

"We do have money to pay for a rental car, so that we can get home to Arizona." She motioned with her head at Gordon, who pulled out the wad of cash. The clerk's eyes took in the large fold of bills.

"I'm sure there is some way we can secure a car with cash. We could pay extra for any potential damages, and we will return it to your Arizona office within three days," Irena vowed. "It would help us out so much."

The young man hesitated, looking from the cash to Irena's face to the computer screen in front of him.

"Perhaps we could talk to your manager?" Irena suggested.

"She isn't here right now. I'm the assistant manager."

"Then you have the power to make this decision," said Irena.

The young man considered. "You will return the car within three days?"

"Yes," said Irena and Gordon in unison.

"I would have to give you our least expensive model," he said, checking the computer screen. "We have a Hyundai."

"That would be perfect," said Irena.

A few minutes later, Gordon eased the Hyundai into traffic and headed for the airport exit. "I'm impressed. But we are going to return this car."

"Of course. Now tell me, why is the SEC after you?"

"Can you punch your address into the GPS. I need to know what freeway to take."

Irena pressed in an address, and a woman's voice began instructing them where to go.

Once on the freeway heading east, Gordon spoke. "The deal I just closed in Vegas. Things seemed off with one of the companies that my contact sold me. He's a gambler, so I should have known better. But the payout was lucrative and hard to ignore."

"One of the first rules of scamming. Too good to be true is too good to be true."

Gordon glanced her way and scowled. "I don't scam people. I manage private equity."

She laughed. "Okay, do you tell the mom and pop companies you're buying—the ones they have slaved to build over generations—that you are going to dismantle them and sell them off like car parts?"

Gordon didn't say anything.

"Let me guess. You pretend like you're going to continue to run those companies."

"I don't say that."

"But you don't not say it, either."

Gordon sighed. "How about we just drive in silence for a while or talk about something else?"

"Like the weather? Thank goodness it's October. The house in Prescott Valley won't be too hot."

"You don't have air-conditioning?"

"I told you. The place is off the grid. I don't pay utilities, so no one can track me."

"What about property tax?"

"The house is in my father's name. One of his many aliases," Irena said quietly. "I vote for driving in silence."

9

After traveling through the hot, desert terrain for some time, Gordon broke the silence, startling Irena out of a half nap.

"My father was a gambler," he said.

She stretched in her seat. "A good gambler or a bad one?"

"Are there good gamblers?" Gordon checked behind the car and eased into another lane to get around a slow-moving truck.

"A good gambler knows to walk away when ahead."

"Okay, a bad gambler. He couldn't walk away from anything."

"Not surprising. Most people aren't good gamblers."

"It was a miserable existence."

Gordon's revelation surprised Irena. She wasn't sure how to respond.

"We were always struggling for money," he continued. "It hit my mother the hardest."

He stole a quick glance her way, meeting her eyes, then refocused on the road.

"I'm listening," she said.

"I have no idea why I'm telling you this. Maybe I think you might understand."

"What it is to live a miserable existence?" Irena asked.

"No. I don't know."

"My father gambled, too—with our livelihood and our safety."

"That must have been difficult."

"It was."

Irena heard a police car siren and swung around to see lights flashing behind them.

"Damnit, I'm not speeding." Gordon pulled the car to the side of the road, tires crunching over gravel. He stopped the car and put his hands on the steering wheel. Irena watched a cop approach in the rearview mirror. When he stood beside the car, Gordon rolled down the window.

"License and registration, please."

Irena reached into the glove box and took out the registration, handing it to him. "This is a rental car, officer."

"And your license?" he addressed Gordon.

"He lost it last night at the blackjack table," Irena said accusingly.

"Is that true, sir?"

Gordon sighed. "Yes. I should have listened when she told me to leave the table and go back to the room. I'll sort out my license as soon as we get home."

"And home is?"

"Arizona."

The officer glanced around the car.

"Can I ask why you stopped us?" Gordon inquired.

"Your back right taillight appears to be out, but that's the rental car company's problem. Make sure to tell them."

"We will, officer," said Irena. "Thank you so much for not fining us."

"Be safe," he said, nodding his head and walking away.

"Either we're extremely lucky, or this is a dream," said Gordon.

"Maybe I'm your good luck charm," said Irena.

Gordon smiled as he eased back onto the freeway. "Maybe."

When they pulled into Irena's driveway three hours later, it was late afternoon, and the sun was beginning its descent. She always felt an uncomfortable knot in her chest when she came here. Sitting at the end of a quiet cul-de-sac, the house looked innocent enough, but the memories flooded back as quickly as Irena shook them away. She fished around in her purse and pulled out a cigarette and lit it. Taking a long drag, she opened the car door and blew the smoke into the air. After several more puffs, she threw the cigarette onto the driveway and stamped it out. "Let's go in."

When they walked into the home in the dimming light, Gordon watched Irena's expression change. It was as if the space held for her some heartache.

"I have a burner phone in the kitchen," she said, walking away from him. "We can charge it in the car and create a hotspot for WIFI. I also filled the generator with gas the last time I was here."

Irena walked over to a bay window next to a small dining area off the kitchen. "I used to have a bird feeder out there. I loved feeding the birds."

Gordon came up beside her to look out at the small backyard and valley beyond dotted with cactus and tumbleweeds. The land had started to redden in the late afternoon sun. Irena shifted and brushed up against him, and he felt electricity between them. She turned to look at him with a tender smile and shy flutter of lashes. Her vulnerability moved Gordon. Taking her by both arms, he drew her gently toward him, kissed first her cheek, then along her neck, breathing the floral scent of her perfume. He looked at her and could see she wanted him. She closed her eyes, and he kissed her. When finally, they pulled apart, Gordon felt a slow, hypnotic warmth enter him, numbing his brain, almost as if this was nothing more than a dream. "I want to make love to you," he breathed, willing himself not to physically sweep her off her feet and go in search of the bedroom. She hesitated, a slight frown between her brows.

He searched her eyes. And then he understood. "Have all your relationships been cons?"

Tears glistened in Irena's eyes, one falling along her cheek. Gordon took her face in his hands and wiped away the tear with his thumb, then kissed where it had been. "You can make this a first time, if you want."

Then she took Gordon's hand and without a word led him down the hall to the last room, turning the handle and pushing the door open to reveal a bed with a silky green bedspread. A clocked ticked on the night-stand and a long antique dresser took up one wall. She pulled back the bedspread and turned to Gordon, slowly unbuttoning his shirt, her fingers working to reveal his chest.

Once done, she let her lips trail across his skin. He pulled her blouse up and over her head, letting her long, dark hair fall back around her bare shoulders, her lacy, black bra pleasing to him. Reaching around, he undid the hooks to reveal ripe, full breasts and pale pink nipples that made his groin swell. He kicked off his shoes, and she unzipped the front of his pants and eased them down, then his shorts. He dropped his shirt to the floor to stand naked before her as if it were a challenge. Then he lay her back on the bed and lifted her skirt, working the gauzy lavender panties down her legs and over her feet. His body burned for hers as he ran his tongue up along the sensitive inside of one leg, licked and teased along the other. Then he pressed his mouth between her legs, running his tongue back and forth over her sweet spot, making her moan. As he kissed and stroked her, he became harder, then rubbed his penis between every sensitive part of her. When she was swollen and moist, he started to straddle her. She put her hand on his chest. "I'll turn over," she said.

Gordon shook his head. "No, I want to see your face; watch you."

Irena started to insist but something inside of her yielded to Gordon's request. She remained silent as he removed her skirt before kissing her deeply. He loved her body, then instructed her, touched and tasted her, until she remembered what true desire felt like. It felt as if she had never been with a man before this. He spoke words softly into her ear, she smelled his salty sweat, felt the damp hair of his chest as it rubbed against her nipples. Then Gordon entered her, his eyes on hers. When she looked away, he gently turned her face back to his. And as his masculine drive exploded deep inside her, she felt as if she would die, digging her nails into the flesh of his back, the sound of their breathing becoming muffled and distant. Afterwards, they lay naked on their backs, side by side, fingers entwined as their heartbeats slowed. He turned his face to hers, and she smiled, shaken, face glowing, already longing for him. He pulled her to him, and they made love again.

10

Irena lay staring at the ceiling as Gordon's breathing slowed and became steady. Being self-conscious with a man was something she hadn't experienced before. But then, she'd never looked into a man's eyes like that. Irena touched her lips where Gordon's lips had been minutes before, then reached down and felt her private area, still wet from her desire. Though he had satiated her, she wished she could have him again now, as if this was indeed the first time she had truly made love to a man. Had Gordon been right, and all the other experiences with men had been cons? The full feeling in her heart told her that might be the case.

She turned and pressed herself up against his long, muscular body, enjoying the feel of her breasts on his hot, sticky skin. She breathed in his musky scent—what she imagined testosterone mixed with sweat smelled like. Gordon shifted then, reaching around with his arm to pull her closer to him. She sighed and decided to take a nap, as well.

When Gordon awoke, the house was black, except for the moonlight streaming in through the gauzy curtains on Irena's windows. He felt himself begin to grow again at the memory of being inside her, when she stirred and reached her hand over. She began to caress him, slowly running her fingertip on the head of his penis.

"I hope you're not teasing me," he said, breaking the silence.

Irena propped herself up on one elbow. "I want to taste you," she said, sending rockets of desire throughout Gordon's body. She burrowed under the covers and began kissing and licking him. Then she raised her head and looked him in the eyes as she pulled back the covers and kneeled over him, her long, black hair covering her breasts. He motioned to reach for her, but she pushed his arms to his sides and smiled, instead guiding him inside of her. Then she moved her hips in a rocking motion, slowly at first, then faster and faster, until Gordon, whose reserves had been used up an hour ago, exploded inside of her. As he cried out her name, she also came. When they had finished and Irena lay on top of him, limp, she murmured, "Oh, my."

Gordon chuckled. "You must be the master of understatement."

Irena kissed the tip of his nose, then slid off Gordon and went over to the dresser. She pulled open a drawer and took out a short nightdress that she slipped over her head. "There is a well, so we have water if you're thirsty."

"I am." Gordon got up and pulled on his pants, leaving his chest bare. "Do you have a flashlight?"

Irena opened another drawer and pulled out two flashlights, handing him one. "Let me lead the way." She headed out of the bedroom.

In the hallway, Irena stopped at the first door to the right, revealing a bathroom. "There's a shower," she said. "Towels are under the sink."

They went several more feet, ignoring a door to the left.

"Was that your father's room?"

Irena swung around, irritation flashing through her eyes in the light coming from Gordon's flashlight. "Why does that matter?"

Gordon realized he'd overstepped a boundary. "Just wondering. That's all."

Irena shifted on one foot uneasily. "Come, I need to turn on the generator in the basement."

They walked into the small kitchen, Gordon's flashlight illuminating the brown linoleum flooring. Irena pulled open the back door and stepped outside into the night. The crescent-shaped moon and sparkling stars filled the black sky. With her flashlight, she located a metal box on the side of the house and flipped on a switch. Then she lit up the basement door next to the house. Gordon reached down and pulled it up, revealing a darkened stairway. When Irena started to head down the steps, he stopped her. "Let me go first, in case a rodent has taken up residence."

She looked like she might protest, then gestured to the stairway. "Be careful on the third step, it's loose."

Gordon descended, flashing the light around when he got to the bottom. A few cardboard boxes and a child's bike. Across the far wall, he spotted the generator.

"It's a good-sized unit," Irena said, walking over to the generator. "We can power it up for an hour or two."

Gordon watched, impressed, as she cranked it to life, then followed her back up the stairs. He reached down and closed the basement door. Then they went back into the kitchen, and Irena flicked the switch on the wall, lighting up the kitchen.

"You're handy in more ways than one," he commented. "Do you cook, too?"

"Only when I have to."

"I love to cook." Gordon took the carton of eggs they'd bought at a minimart before arriving at the house out of the bag, along with tortillas and beans, and got to work.

Irena watched Gordon move about the kitchen, as if she were watching a movie. No one had ever made her a meal. Bought her food, yes, but not cooked for her. While she enjoyed the view of his bare chest and his cooking prowess, she also began to experience the familiar, dreaded sense of unease that plagued her whenever she came back to this house.

"You only need to talk to the man, Irena. Keep him busy while I get the account numbers from his computer. Then we can leave."

"He makes my skin crawl, Dad. Last time he put his hand on my thigh. And he smells like mothballs."

"You'll be fine tonight. Wear pants, and when he goes to touch you, move away. I'll be nearby. I promise I'll make it quick. He won't have a chance to do anything. Once we get this payout, there will be enough money to buy that house. How does that sound?"

Irena smiled. "Really good. You're talking about the house we looked at the other day at the end of the cul-de-sac?"

"Yes. You liked it, didn't you?"

Irena nodded vigorously.

"I'll get a real job, and you can go to school and ride a bike in the neighborhood. And make friends."

"What will you do for work?"

Her father adjusted his bowtie in the dingy mirror of their motel room, then patted his unruly brown hair and swung around to face her. "Maybe I'll buy myself an ice cream truck. Wouldn't that be fun? You can ride around all day with me selling ice cream. Of course, we'll have to make sure not to eat all the profits."

"I'll be in school, Dad."

He hit the side of his head with his hand. "That's right. After school, then."

Irena tried to imagine her father working in an ice cream truck, or any job, and she just couldn't.

11

"We only lived here for three years," said Irena, after taking a bite of her burrito. "When I was fifteen, sixteen, and seventeen."

Gordon looked up from his food. "Where did you live before?"

"Nowhere," she said, directing her attention to her burrito. The unwanted lump in her throat had started to expand. "Forget I said anything," she managed to say. "This place makes me maudlin." She expected an awkward silence, but Gordon pushed back his chair and came around the table, stopping to stand next to her. She looked up at him, confused.

"Stand up," he said gently.

Irena did so, unsure of what he wanted. He shocked her by taking her into his arms. To her horror, she began sobbing and couldn't stop. As she let out emotions that had been pent up for years, Gordon rubbed her back. Finally, when the tears subsided, he loosened his grip. "Let's get out of here as soon as possible."

Gordon held Irena while she cried, pushing away his own unpleasant family memories. Feelings of rage and disdain as his father told another stupid story about what went wrong at the blackjack tables. Watching his mother pull from her secret stash of money she earned mending clothing so she could go to the all-night market and buy Gordon and his sister food for school lunches the next day.

When Irena went to get her burner phone and returned, he noted that she must have made up her face. The red blotches were gone, and her eyes appeared less puffy. She handed him a cellphone and charger.

"If you plug it in while the generator is on, you should be able to get a hotspot for your laptop," she told him.

He set up in the kitchen, first ensuring he had a secure connection before checking his accounts. Nothing frozen yet. Whatever the suits had wanted to talk to him about, it hadn't advanced too far. He dialed Benson Holmes, his connection at the NSA.

"I thought that might be you," Benson said when he heard Gordon's voice. "There's been some chatter."

"About?"

"You asked me about that woman. I dumped her phone and got more info about who might be after her. But the chatter is about you."

"Involving the SEC?"

"You heard?"

"I saw them waiting for me at the airport, so I split."

"They wanted to know about Ray Goldstein. Didn't you recently broker a deal with him in Vegas?"

"A big one."

"He's being indicted."

"Dammit."

"Just get ahead of this. Call the SEC tomorrow. They've frozen all his assets, which will include your deals with him, but I would think you can get your money back, if you play your cards right. Sorry, Vegas humor." Benson chuckled. "Hey, whose phone is this?"

"It belongs to a friend. I'm helping her out."

"Since when does the perpetual bachelor help women out?"

Gordon glanced at Irena washing the dishes.

"Does this woman have something on you?"

"No, nothing like that. I'm fine." Gordon assured him.

His friend was silent. Finally, he said, "It's your life, but I'd get ahold of the SEC pronto. Let me give you the information I got about who has been calling Miss AKA. I think you'll find that these details will give you a really good reason to finish up whatever it is you're doing with her."

As Irena stood at the sink, she watched Gordon from the corner of her eye. She liked how he smiled so easily when he talked to people, and how often he laughed. When he hung up the phone, he made another call. She turned off the tap and took a dishtowel out of a drawer, moving quietly so she could hear his conversation.

"Angela, it's me. Can you keep Trixie for another few days? I'll explain later."

Irena froze. Of course, he had people who meant something to him. She was foolish to think this was anything but an arrangement. She rubbed a plate vigorously. What an idiot she had been to show such vulnerability. As she reached for another dish to dry, Gordon ended the call.

"I have some information on who is trying to find you," he said.

Irena's back was to Gordon. She took a deep breath, willing herself to stay cool, but a dam broke. Whirling around, she exclaimed, "You're married? And you have a child? You should have told me!"

Gordon leaned back in his chair and grinned.

In response, Irena slammed the plate on the edge of the Formica countertop, sending bits of glass flying. Pain shot through her hand, and she looked at her palm as blood oozed from it. Gordon jumped up to help, but she yelled, "Stay away from me."

"That was my sister, Angela, and Trixie is my Shih Tzu," said Gordon. "Sit down so I can check out your hand."

"Your sister and dog?" Irena's face colored. She leaned against the counter while Gordon examined her hand, dabbing the blood with the dishtowel. "Keep pressure on it while I clean up this mess."

Irena watched as Gordon got rid of the results of her temper tantrum, unsure what to say. Finally, she decided it was best to say nothing.

When the glass was cleaned up, he asked, "Do you have any bandages?"

Irena motioned to leave the room, but Gordon said, "I'll get them. Just tell me where."

"In the medicine cabinet in the bathroom." Gordon started to walk away, and she said, "I'm sorry."

"I shouldn't have taken what you said so lightly," he said quietly. "Not after the way…"

"What?"

"Your father treated you."

"My father treated me just fine," said Irena, standing up straighter. "I'm tired, that's all."

Gordon went to the bathroom and pulled open the medicine cabinet, his eyes falling on pain reliever, antacid, a box of bandages and several prescription bottles. He glanced toward the open bathroom door, then checked out the name on the bottles. Walter Martin. That must be Irena's father. As he examined the labels of each bottle, his heart quickened.

12

When he returned to the kitchen, Irena was sitting in a chair, staring straight ahead. He pulled up a seat next to her and took her hand in his. After checking and seeing no fragments of glass, he applied a bandage.

"Now that I've made a fool of myself, how long have you had Trixie?"

Gordon smiled. "She's four years old. I got her from a good friend of mine, a breeder. She and her husband talked me into taking her home."

"That's nice of your sister to watch her. Are you guys close?"

"Sort of," Gordon said. "She doesn't agree with my line of work. She's a bleeding-heart liberal. Works as a pro bono lawyer helping the indigent. We have a lot of debates centered around capitalism."

Irena smiled, imagining the lively dinner conversations. "It must be nice to have a sibling. I always wished I had a brother."

"Not a sister?"

Irena shook her head. "A brother would have been more useful to ward off the bullies."

That surprised Gordon. "You were bullied?"

"Terribly."

"I can't imagine anyone pushing you around."

"I learned to take care of myself. Mostly I was teased about my father. And the way we lived."

An awkward silence ensued, which Gordon finally broke. "I have some information on who is stalking you."

Irena's eyebrows raised.

"The Lithuanian mafia mean anything to you?"

He watched terror replace curiosity in her eyes. "I paid them. They said they'd leave us alone," she said.

"Us?"

Irena tore her eyes from his. "What about you and the SEC? Shouldn't you be working on that?"

Gordon took Irena's chin in his fingers, urging her to look him in the eyes. "If I'm going to help you, I need to know who else is involved."

She sighed, her shoulders slumping. Gordon removed his hand from her chin and waited.

"It was our last heist, I guess you could say, before my father disappeared. I thought when I paid them what we'd stolen, he'd come back."

"When was the last time you saw him?"

"Three years ago, in a bar in Eastern Europe." Irena stopped, the memory slapping her across the face again. "There's no point in talking about this."

"There is. You say you paid them, but they think otherwise."

"I did pay them! Then I went to an apartment in Warsaw where they said my father would be, but he wasn't there."

"What happened the last time you saw your father in the bar?"

"He was with these two men. Lithuanians. They had guns under their jackets. Dad tried to pretend he was okay, but I could tell he was frightened. He told me to transfer funds from his emergency account overseas and gave me some account information for transferring. Then they made him leave with them."

"And you paid them?"

"Yes, I did exactly what he told me to do."

"What are the chances of your father being alive?"

Irena put her fingers on her temples and shook her head. "I thought I'd found something a couple of months ago that might lead me to him. I had a hacker—." Irena gasped. "That little sneak. I had a hacker, who came highly recommended, decrypt some files that I'd hoped could lead me to my father, but it was a dead end. We met in a coffee shop. She...Dammit. I should have paid her."

"You didn't pay her?"

"I didn't have any cash. My latest mark was on to me, and so I had to move quick. I bought her a cup of coffee. The whole transaction only took her five minutes."

"What's her name?"

Irena struggled to remember. "She looked like a little blonde Raggedy Ann doll."

"Who referred her?"

"My friend Hermann." She turned on her phone and began scrolling through her contacts. "We've known each other for years and pull each other out of tight spots."

Gordon was about to ask her what sort of tight spots but decided against it.

Irena dialed her friend. "It's me on a burner. Call me back." When she hung up, she said, "It could be five minutes or five days before I hear from him." She yawned.

"Maybe we should get some sleep and hit this again first thing in the morning." Gordon stood up, suddenly feeling a heavy weight of fatigue.

"We need to turn off the generator, or there won't be any gas left."

"I'll get it," said Gordon, heading for the basement, grabbing a flashlight off the kitchen counter on his way out. When he got into the small space and the light hit the bike, he examined it. Had Irena ever even ridden it? He tried to picture her as a young girl, but had a hard time doing so. Was it because she'd apparently never been allowed to have a childhood? He turned off the switch on the generator and climbed the stairs to a dark house.

In the bedroom, he found Irena lying on the left side of the bed, her hair splayed out on the pillow. He usually slept on the left but decided not to say anything. After undressing, he slipped into bed next to her. She was so quiet, he wondered if she was awake.

"Thank you for turning off the generator."

"Mmm hmm," Gordon murmured, pulling her to him. He smiled when she sighed and scooted even closer to him.

"You said you wanted a bike, so I got you one!"

"You took it from the girl down the street, Dad. I can't ride it in this neighborhood."

"I guess neighborhood living is going to take some getting used to." Her father was studying the paper. "Just tell her you got the same bike for your birthday. There's no crime in that."

"There is if it is the same bike. And my birthday is in November. It's March."

Her father looked up. "Patsy 50 or Lightning Strikes Twice?"

"What?"

"Which one do you think is going to win? You're better at determining the odds than me."

"We have to pay the mortgage next week, Dad. You can't spend it on gambling."

"Give me a break, will you? The normie life is going to take some getting used to. I need exciting hobbies."

Irena grabbed the race day program from her father and checked the stats on the horses.

"Patsy 50," she said. "And your limit is fifty dollars."

Irena woke in the middle of the night and strained to listen. Was that a sound in the living room? She sat up, her heart banging in her chest. Holding her breath, she waited. Silence, except for a coyote baying in the nearby foothills. Lying back down and pressing her back against Gordon's broad chest, his steady heartbeat soon lulled her back to sleep.

13

When Gordon awoke the next morning, Irena's side of the bed was empty. He stretched and listened. All quiet. He got up and slid on his pants, then made his way into the kitchen. Empty. No one in the small living room, either. Just as anxiety began to nip at him, he spied her through the bay window. Walking over, he looked outside. She wore her nightdress and was barefoot, her glossy hair glinting in the morning sun. Ripples of pleasure ran through his body as he remembered being with her.

She reached down and picked up some stones and threw them across the yard. Then she raised her face to the sunny sky and smiled. At that moment, Gordon realized he had never seen her smile like that. Grin, yes, but not smile. When she saw him through the window, his heart skipped a few beats, then her smile widened in greeting, and she waved him outside.

The air was warm and crisp, the sky a bright blue. A bird flew out of a giant cactus. Gordon watched it flap away.

"October is one of the most beautiful months in Arizona," she said. "How did you sleep?"

"Good." He eyed her. "You look more rested than yesterday. How long have you been up?"

"About an hour. I heard from Hermann. Let's have something to eat, and I'll tell you how our conversation went."

In the kitchen, Irena pointed to a chair. "Sit down, and I'll make you some breakfast."

Gordon waited while she opened a cupboard and pulled out two bowls, spoons, and a box of cereal. He laughed.

"I told you I wasn't a cook," she said, placing Cheerios onto the table. "And I can't guarantee these aren't stale. How much cereal shall I pour you, sir?" she asked, hovering the box over his bowl.

Gordon drew her to him, enjoying the feel of her soft body against his. "I've got a better idea for breakfast," he said, putting his hand underneath her nightdress and fondling her breasts, the nipples tightening at his touch.

"As much as I like the idea of you ravishing me right here," she leaned down and placed her soft lips on his. "Hermann will be here soon, so we better eat while we can."

"Here?" Gordon wasn't liking the sound of this. Besides the visit being an exposure risk, he wondered just how close these two were.

"I told you, he's cool. We've known each other since high school." Irena pulled a box of soy milk out of the bag of groceries from the mini-mart and opened it. She poured some over the cereal in their bowls and sat down to eat.

"And you're just friends?" Gordon couldn't believe he'd just revealed himself like that.

Irena looked up from her bowl, surprise registering on her face. She swallowed. "Please, no more broken dishes." Grinning, she took another bite.

"What kind of work have you done together?" Gordon continued probing.

"I'm a much naughtier girl than Hermann. He actually makes a real living as a barista, but he runs in certain circles and is up for a con now and then."

Just then there was a rapping on the door.

"That must be him." Irena hopped up and started heading for the front of the house.

"Hold on. You don't know for sure that's him, and shouldn't you get dressed?"

Irena giggled. "No, but you should. If you insist on being my bodyguard, then come with me."

At the door, Gordon stopped her. "Check through the peephole, and if it's him and only him, let him in."

Irena peered through the hole, then pulled the door open. Gordon watched as Irena embraced a tall, well-built blond, who looked like he'd just stepped out of a suntan commercial. When they pulled apart, Hermann eyed Gordon and put his hands on his hips. "Who is this delicious-looking man, Irena?"

Irena turned, and introduced Gordon. "Put your eyes back in your head, Hermann. I'm sure Brad wouldn't appreciate you ogling Gordon."

"Can't blame me for looking!"

Irena gave him a good-natured slap on the arm as he reached out to shake Gordon's hand.

"Very nice to meet you," said Gordon.

"Now that everyone has met, let's sit down in the kitchen," said Irena. "We just finished breakfast. I cooked."

"Now that's something I want to see," said Hermann as they headed inside. "I made all of our late-night snacks when we were kids. Remember my fabulous s'mores, Irena? The peanut butter was the secret ingredient," he told Gordon as they sat down. "We used to console ourselves with goodies when we were supposed to be doing our dreaded homework."

After they all got comfortable, Irena began explaining about the texts she'd been receiving. "Remember that hacker you gave me the name of? The blond woman?"

"Sammy?"

"I think she's mixed up in this somehow. I had her unencrypt some files that I thought might lead me to my father. It ended up a dead end in terms of finding him, but the accounts involved the Lithuanian mafia. She had to transfer the files onto her computer to unencrypt them. I told her to erase them, but I think she kept a copy."

Hermann shifted in his seat. "Irena, you know the Lithuanian mafia is hardcore. This is out of your league. And why would Sammy keep the files?"

"I might not have paid her for her services."

"Irena!" Hermann admonished.

"Someone was after me, and I had to get out of there fast."

Hermann looked to Gordon, as if to garner his support, then back to Irena. "Sweets, you don't even know if your father is alive."

Irena pushed her chair back from the kitchen table and stood up. "I would feel it if he was dead."

Her words hung in the air. Hermann took the cereal box and sprinkled some Cheerios into his palm and ate them.

"Do you know this Sammy very well?" Gordon asked Hermann.

"I know of her reputation, which is stellar. Although, since you stiffed her, I wouldn't put it past her to check out the files."

"Assuming Irena's father is alive, it would help us to talk to Sammy and find out what she did with the files," said Gordon.

Hermann nodded and pulled out his cellphone, then typed in a text. "She's pretty responsive. In the meantime," he squeezed Irena's arm, "tell me where you've been hiding him."

"We've known each other for a couple of days now." Irena picked up her cereal bowl and drank the remaining milk.

Hermann looked surprised. "That's all? I'd swear you'd known each other for months."

Irena was about to respond when Hermann's phone buzzed. He checked the screen. "It's her boyfriend." He answered the phone. "Twitch. What are you doing answering your better half's phone?" After listening for a moment, he sat up in his chair abruptly, causing the milk in Gordon's cereal bowl to slosh. "When?"

Hermann hung up the phone, his bright smile gone. "Sammy is missing. Twitch found her VW Bug in front of their apartment last night. The door to her car was wide open, her stuff spilled out all over the place, and she's nowhere to be found."

14

Both Gordon and Hermann looked to Irena.

"What?" she said. "Sammy is a hacker. She probably made plenty of enemies."

Gordon turned back to Hermann. "Can you give us her boyfriend's contact information?"

Hermann nodded. "He's in Long Beach," he said, texting the information to their burner phone. Then he said to Irena, "I'd say I could help, but it seems to me that Gordon can handle you, which means he can handle just about anything. Besides, I need to get back."

"Thanks for the information," said Irena as she walked him to the front door. Hermann turned to her. "Just be careful, okay? You're the only friend I kept from high school."

Irena laughed. "I was the only friend you had in high school."

Hermann took on a mock expression of insult. "Not true. Me and the principal were best buds. I spent every other week in his office." Hermann's expression became more serious. "I mean it, sweets." He glanced Gordon's way. "Take care of my girl." Then he slipped out the front door.

Irena turned to Gordon. "Time to pack up?"

"One thing first. You might not want to do this, but we need to check out your father's room. See if it holds any clues."

Irena sighed.

"I can go in and look around if you don't want to."

She squared her shoulders. "No, that's okay, we can both go in." She walked down the hall, Gordon following, and stopped in front of her father's bedroom door. Taking a deep breath, she turned the handle. Locked.

"This doesn't surprise me," she said, going down the hall to her bedroom to get a hairpin. She used it to undo the lock. Easing the door open, she reached around and flicked on the lights.

The room was in a shambles. Stacks of newspapers lined the floor, and there were piles of them on the bed.

Irena made her way through the rubble to her father's desk. She picked up a book that lay open, noting that it was about cryptocurrency.

Gordon came up behind her. "Interesting choice of reading material."

"The plan with the Lithuanian con had been that we would put the windfall in cryptocurrency, then disappear."

"Disappear?"

"My dad was tired of what he called the normie life. He wanted to buy his own island and live on it. I went along with him, but I just wanted the money."

"For what?"

"What do you mean?"

"Everyone has a reason for wanting a lot of money."

Irena thought about it. "Because you can use it to buy whatever you want." She flipped through the book, finding a credit card tucked in the pages, which she slid into her bra. "It buys power." Her eye caught what looked like an airline ticket. She flipped back to the page in the book and pulled out two tickets. One for her alias, Kezia, and one for her father's alias, Homer.

"Belize," she said, checking the date. Three weeks before her father disappeared. She turned around to look Gordon in the eye. "And why do you like money?"

Gordon looked uncomfortable. "It buys help when you need it."

That puzzled Irena. "For your father's gambling debts?"

"Oh, hell, no. Not his debts."

"Then what does he need?"

"A miracle. He has Alzheimer's. I have a friend from college, a neurologist who's been studying the disease. I've been helping fund his research."

"Is it working?"

"There's a drug trial coming that may. My mom's really counting on it. Despite all the crap my father put her through during their marriage, she still loves him."

"Well, I hope your neurologist friend can help," Irena said. "I never knew my mother. She died when I was two. A car accident." Before Gordon could ask any questions, she continued. "We better get on the road."

"We have to turn the rental car in," Gordon reminded her.

"I'm a step ahead of you. There's a car in the garage. My old Volvo. It should get us where we want to go."

Two hours later after packing up and returning the rental car, they were speeding down the I-10, heading for California. Since he'd confided in Irena about his parents, Gordon had been quiet. Irena broke the silence. "How'd you end up doing the work you do?"

Gordon adjusted the car's rearview mirror. "I had always planned on running the family business. We had a large manufacturing company that produced many kinds of plastics."

"Had?"

"The business was started by my grandfather on my mother's side. My mom helped run the company for many years. My father acted as CEO for a time, but his gambling got in the way. So, the plan was for me and Mom to run the company together. She had the technical expertise, and I had the business acumen."

"But your father got sick."

Gordon nodded as he floored the Volvo to get around a large truck. "For the first few years, she took care of him herself while also working at the business, but he became a full-time job. We were planning on hiring someone to replace her at the company, but then we got a lucrative offer for the business and decided to take it. During negotiations, I realized that I had a flair for buying and selling companies."

"Do you enjoy your work?"

"I find it satisfying to close a good deal, and I'm very good at it. So, yes, I'd say I do enjoy it."

Irena thought about what Gordon said in the silence that ensued. How did she feel about the cons that had run her life for so long? In many ways, it was addictive. The rush to see if she could get what she wanted from someone. But the buzz always wore off. And the cons could have consequences.

"Dad, the man had an accent. We don't speak Polish or Lithuanian. We're way out of our league here."

"We'll be fine. I have it on good authority that the man pays well. Then we can buy our island. No more cons. We'll spend our days picking coconuts and fishing for our meals."

"You don't even like fish."

"I'll make myself like fish. You'll see."

15

Irena had nodded off, her head against the car window. What was she dreaming about, Gordon wondered, or was she even dreaming? He thought about how quickly her moods had swung at her house when faced with all her family memories. His own father had been a pain in the ass most of the time, but at least he'd been predictable. It looked to Gordon like every day had been a different day for Irena growing up.

When they crossed into California, Gordon pulled off the highway to get some gas. As he drove into the station, Irena stirred and yawned.

"I can drive, you know."

"I like to drive," answered Gordon. "It calms me."

He felt Irena's eyes on him as he eased the car next to a gas pump and shut off the engine. "I can hear you thinking. Is there a question in there?" He turned to face her.

"No, it's just that you seem pretty calm most of the time."

"I'll take that as a compliment." Gordon reached into his pocket and pulled out some cash for gas. "There's a McDonald's over there." He gestured. "We can grab something to eat."

Irena shook her head vigorously, surprising Gordon. "My father loved McDonalds," she said, staring at the building and its big yellow arches. "We did a lot of cons there when I was a kid."

"We can eat wherever you want," Gordon said quietly.

After they bought Mexican food and were sitting in the parking lot eating, Gordon said, "If you want to talk about it…"

Irena set down her taco and sighed. "My father was complicated."

"I'm seeing that." Gordon took a pull on his soda. "When I went to get you a bandage at your house, I saw prescriptions in the medicine cabinet. I imagine his condition had something to do with him being so complicated?"

"Especially when he didn't take his medicine, which he hated, because it made him sleepy," she said. "Then the mania would start, and the cons would get even more intense and crazy."

"Hell of a way to grow up," said Gordon.

Irena gazed out the window. "Yes, it was."

After they finished eating, Gordon turned on the car and let it idle. "Four more hours and we'll be in Long Beach. Have you gotten any more texts?"

Irena pulled her bag from the floor and set it on her lap, digging around until she found the phone. She turned it on and waited. When she gasped, Gordon held out his hand for her phone. He glanced at the screen. *You think you can run to California, but you can't hide.* He handed it back to her.

"Answer," he said.

"What?"

"They're obviously tracking us. We need to know more."

"How about: *I know who this is. Let's meet?*"

"That sounds good to me."

A minute went by. No answer.

"Better to turn it off now," said Gordon. "You've got whoever it is wondering."

Irena nodded and switched off the phone. "We should change vehicles."

"I saw a few clunkers at the gas station." Gordon headed back to the garage, where a mechanic worked under a suspended car.

He and Irena got out and approached, the mechanic not noticing them until they were a few feet away. Setting down a wrench, he silenced the Mexican pop tune coming out of a grimy boombox. Then he pulled a bandana out of his back pocket and wiped his brow. "We're closing soon. Something wrong with your car?"

"Actually, we need a trade in," said Irena.

The man eyed the Volvo. "I don't need any trouble."

"The car is mine, and it's in good shape. I just don't want to be seen driving it anymore," she told him. "You can chop it up for parts or paint it. Do whatever you want. Straight trade."

The mechanic considered. "All I got is a Honda. A little beat up, but it drives." They followed him to a back lot, where he pointed to a steel gray car with a dented bumper.

"Perfect," said Gordon. He glanced at Irena, who stood there staring at her Volvo.

"Just give me a minute to mentally say goodbye," she said. "I worked my senior year in high school at the coffee shop with Hermann to buy her."

When they pulled into Long Beach nearly four hours later, they followed Twitch's directions to a condo complex. After parking in a guest space, they climbed stairs to a second-floor door. Gordon rapped three times, then the door opened to reveal a guy with shaggy brown hair and worried eyes. He ushered them into a bright living room with a plush, turquoise couch and pink Chinese lantern hanging from the ceiling. On the coffee table lay a half-eaten burrito.

"Sammy's decorating," said Twitch. Then he faced Irena. "So, you're the woman who got her into this mess?"

Gordon saw Irena's spine tighten and gave her a warning look. "We don't know that for sure," he said. "But if that's the case, Irena is sorry."

"I should have paid her that day in the coffee shop. I was being pursued, and I didn't have any cash," said Irena. "We're here to help. Do you have her computer?"

Twitch considered for a moment, then shuffled to a back room and returned with a pink laptop. He motioned for them to sit down on the couch. Then he opened the computer and tapped something in, handing it to Gordon.

Irena sat down next to Gordon as he pulled up the computer's file directory. "We're looking for anything mentioning Lithuania, correct?"

"Yes."

After some more typing, a spreadsheet sprang up. "Does this look familiar?"

Irena leaned over Gordon. "That's the information."

"But you said these didn't lead you anywhere?"

"Not to my father, but they did lead me to a bank account in the Cayman's."

"So, that's what this is about. They want their money back."

Irena shifted uncomfortably. "Possibly."

"How much?"

Irena was silent.

"How much, Irena?"

"Thirty million, okay. I've been holding onto it, hoping I could use it to trade for my father."

"You need to give that money back so I can get my girl back," cried Twitch, whose phone buzzed. He answered as he walked toward the back of the apartment. "No, nothing yet," Irena heard him say into the phone.

After Twitch was out of earshot, Gordon turned to Irena, his eyes boring into hers. "The money is in your offshore account?"

She nodded.

"We need to tell them you've got the money in exchange for Sammy, and your father. But not from here. We can't compromise Twitch's whereabouts."

Just then an email popped up on the screen. Gordon clicked on it, and they both read it.

Irena gasped. "Oh, my God." She glanced toward the hallway. "Do you think Twitch knows?"

"From the sound of this email, Sammy may not even know for sure," said Gordon.

Irena read the email again. *Congratulations. Test results show that you're pregnant. Please call to set up a prenatal exam as soon as possible.*

16

Irena leaned back on the couch. An innocent baby's life on the line wasn't something she'd bargained for. Glancing back to the bedroom, she whispered, "I don't think we should tell him."

Gordon replied, "If I was him, I'd want to know."

Irena sat up, reaching for her purse.

"What are you doing?"

"I need some air."

Gordon took ahold of her arm and held it stationary. "Try to focus. There are two lives on the line now."

Irena shrugged off his hand. "Okay, fine."

Twitch returned, looking at them hopefully. "Anything?"

Gordon motioned to the empty armchair. "You better sit down."

Twitch suddenly looked like he might cry.

"It's not bad news," said Gordon. "Just sit."

He slouched into the chair. "Okay, spill."

Gordon cleared his throat. "When we were checking Sammy's computer, an email popped up." He handed the computer to Twitch, who took a few seconds before he checked out the screen. His eyes widened. "Sammy's pregnant?"

"So, this *is* a surprise," said Gordon.

"She wasn't feeling good lately, but I thought it was something she ate." The confusion on Twitch's face turned to resolve. "We gotta find her."

"No word about her at all?" Irena asked, sitting up straighter.

"I was just talking to a guy in the FBI me and Sammy do some work for. Hopefully he can help."

"Good to have the FBI on your side," said Gordon.

"All I want is my girl back." Twitch stood up and pulled a packet of cigarettes out of his pocket.

"Can I have one?" asked Irena.

"I don't know. Can you find Sammy? It's you who got her kidnapped in the first place."

"Let's all calm down," said Gordon. "None of this is going to help find Sammy."

Twitch sighed and threw the packet towards Irena, who caught it in midair.

"First things first," said Gordon. "We need to make a call that won't be traced to this location. We may be able to communicate with the kidnappers."

"Okay, let's go," Twitch said.

"You should stay here in case your friend at the FBI shows or Sammy calls. We'll come back right away."

Twitch sat and buried his head in his hands.

Losing the urge to smoke, Irena set the pack down on the coffee table. She reached out and gave Twitch's arm a reassuring pat, then left the room without saying anything.

In the car, Irena pulled out the cellphone.

"Let's wait until we're driving," said Gordon. "It's a lot harder to track a moving target."

When they were on the freeway speeding south in the fast lane, Irena powered the phone on.

"No texts." She noted, then typed a text and read it to Gordon. "*I've got your money. I want the girl and my father.*"

"That should do it." Gordon nodded.

A text came back almost immediately after she pushed send. *"What girl?"*

"How about, you know what girl. And I want my father, too," suggested Gordon.

Irena tapped it in, then waited and read the return text, *"We'll find you. You know that."*

She started to enter a reply demanding they return her father, but Gordon stopped her. "Turn it off."

"Why?"

"I can feel you becoming agitated. It's obvious you're not going to get a straight answer."

Irena was about to protest, but realized Gordon was right. This wasn't the time to misstep and show her hand. She shut off the phone as Gordon exited the freeway and got back on, heading in the opposite direction. "Do you think they have Sammy?" she asked him.

"I'm not sure. We need a cyber expert to do a trace on the phone to see if we can get some information on where the texts are coming from."

When they returned to Twitch's apartment, a man in jeans and a t-shirt opened the door. Despite his casual attire, Irena guessed from his no-nonsense stance that he was Twitch's FBI contact. "Twitch tells me you are involved in Sammy's disappearance," he said, surveying them both, then glancing behind them.

Irritation swept through Irena. "That's us. Although, we don't know for sure who took Sammy. She did hack for a living."

The man's stance softened, and he stood back so they could enter the apartment. "Duly noted."

At a nearby table sat a young woman, who was checking out Sammy's computer. As Gordon and Irena sat down, the man introduced himself. "I'm Special Agent Tony Molinaro. Me and Twitch go way back, so I'm here to help, although my time is limited." His eyes fell on Irena. "How about you tell me what you know. All of it."

Irena leaned back on the couch and relayed how she'd been trying to locate her father when she called Sammy, and how Sammy appeared to have kept the files.

"You have any Lithuanian contact names?" Tony asked.

"Just a phone number. Can you trace the source of recent texts?"

"They're likely using a burner, but it's worth a try." Tony took the phone from Irena and handed it to the woman, who nodded. "You never talked to someone in person?" he added.

Irena considered his question. "Once. When I arrived in Warsaw to try and retrieve my father."

"How'd the person get ahold of you?"

Irena thought back. "If I remember correctly, a woman called me on the hotel room phone. She gave me the name of a bar and told me to go there. My father was there with two men when I arrived."

Tony dialed a number. "Give me the hotel name, dates of your stay, and the name you used when you checked in."

While they waited, Irena willed herself not to think about her father. The best thing she could do right now was accept the fact that he might already be dead. Just then, Gordon covered her hand with his and squeezed. She gave him a sidelong glance and smiled.

Tony hung up the phone. "Anything there, Cathy?"

The young woman shook her head and got up and handed the phone back to Irena. "It's a burner, like we thought."

"Well my contact in Warsaw was able to pull up where that hotel call originated. An accounting firm owned by Solana Petrauskas. Does that name mean anything to you?"

Irena thought for a moment. "No, it doesn't ring a bell."

Tony's phone buzzed, and he checked the screen. "I've got a photo I want you to check out." He handed his phone to her.

Irena did a double take when she looked at the photo of the woman, with her dark raven hair hanging down in a large braid and blood red lipstick. It was the woman she'd seen her father with several times over the years.

"Who is she?" Irena asked as Gordon took the phone and had a look.

"You've seen her before?" Tony asked.

"Yes, a few times with my father. But here in the States."

"You're looking at Solana Petrauskas, the leader of an extremely dangerous Lithuanian mob," said Tony. "They smuggle all sorts of illegal items, including weapons and explosives. She's also wanted for arson."

17

Irena didn't usually find herself speechless, but this information had her mute. Her father associating with a cartel that smuggled explosives and weapons? She had always thought that his schemes had been small time.

"I've got someone tracking Solana as we speak," Tony continued. "Tell me about the last time you saw her."

Irena hesitated.

"A woman's life is on the line, and her unborn child. Now is not the time to hide things, Ms. Martin." Tony kept his eyes on her face.

Irena sighed. "My father and I were in Vegas on a con. It was a couple of months before he disappeared. He had bought some glass collectibles from a lady for cheap, but they were worth a fortune. He was looking for a buyer. He tried to get Solana to help sell them."

"How did you meet up with her?"

"We were at a buffet at the Bellagio, and she walked up. I could tell my father knew she was coming, though. That's the way it usually was with her. She'd show up, and he'd pretend it was a coincidence."

"How'd their conversation go?"

"She said hello to me, then started to argue with my father about his latest con. She said the glass collectibles weren't worth anything. They squabbled about that during the whole dinner."

Irena stopped talking and reached for the packet of cigarettes on the coffee table, lighting one. She took a toke and blew out the smoke. "My father is…was troubled, but we never did anything that would jeopardize people's lives. This is the first time I'm hearing about explosives and weapons. He never even owned a gun. It sounds odd, but my father prided himself on not using force during a con."

Gordon spoke up. "Maybe that's why they were arguing that night."

Irena felt so confused, and her head had begun to ache.

Gordon watched Irena's face. She hid it well, but after spending the last few days with her, he knew when she had been pushed to the edge. She began blinking more than usual. Most likely to keep tears at bay.

Just then Sammy's phone rang on the coffee table, its ring tone a screaming heavy metal tune. Twitch sprinted into the living room from the back of the apartment. "What should I do?"

Tony held up a finger. "Cathy. You ready?"

The agent addressed Twitch. "Keep them on the line for at least a minute."

Twitch grabbed the phone and answered, pressing speaker phone. "Sammy?"

"I'm not Sammy, but maybe I'll let you talk to her," said a woman's voice that Irena recognized as Solana's.

Twitch ran his hand through his hair. "Okay, sure, whatever you want. Just let me talk to Sammy."

"Shut up and listen. Your girlfriend has some passcodes in her computer that I need. Give them to me, and then I'll let her go."

Irena sat up. Gordon squeezed her hand to stop her from saying anything.

"We can make a trade," said Twitch. "The passwords for Sammy. Where are you?"

"I'll be in touch." Then she hung up.

"A few more seconds, and I would have had her," said Cathy. "The signal was pinging off cell towers all over the place, so I have no idea where she was calling from."

"Now what?" Twitch cried. "We don't even know where to go and get her."

"Take some deep breaths," said Tony. "The woman wants her money. She'll call back." Tony turned to Irena. "Did that sound like Solana's voice?"

"I think so."

"You're not sure?"

"There was a lot of background noise, but I'd say that I'm ninety-nine percent sure."

"We can't just sit here!" exploded Twitch.

"We're not going to do that," said Tony. "She'll call back, and Cathy will figure out where she's calling from. Then we'll go and get Sammy."

"What about my father…" Irena said.

"He's been missing for three years. There's a good chance he's not alive. I'm sorry," said Tony.

Irena stood up. "Since it doesn't appear that you need us anymore, can we go?"

Tony thought for a second. "Sure. But let me know where you'll be."

Once outside in the car, Irena behind the wheel this time, Gordon spoke. "What are you up to?"

"Up to?"

"I can see your wheels spinning."

Irena was silent for a minute. "I know where Solana was calling from. Near the Bellagio, in Vegas."

"How do you know?"

"I heard the water show in the background. Solana insisted we go see it that night after dinner. I say we go back to Vegas and find Sammy ourselves. And who knows, maybe we'll find my dad, too," she said hopefully.

Gordon thought through his next words carefully before he spoke. "Are you sure you want to do this? Solana sounds dangerous."

"She's holding Sammy hostage, and it's all my fault. For all I know, she could be holding my father. I need to do this. You don't have to go if you don't want to. I know you need to deal with the whole SEC thing. I've kept you from that long enough."

"How about this. Let's find a pay phone. I can make a call to the SEC, and then we head to Vegas."

At a gas station down the street from Twitch's house, Gordon spotted a pay phone and went to make a call. Irena waited in the car while he dialed the number to the SEC Office of Investigations. A woman answered.

"This is Gordon Bradshaw. I'm currently away on vacation, but I heard someone from your office was attempting to get ahold of me."

The woman put him on hold, then returned a short time later. "Mr. Bradshaw, we did need to speak with you a couple of days ago, but the case has been transferred to the Department of Justice. You're being advised to cut your vacation short and report to one of their offices immediately. You're now a person of interest in a possible crime."

Gordon felt his chest constricting. "I don't understand. What or who does this have to do with?"

"I can't tell you much, but I can tell you that we originally contacted you to discuss a recent transaction between you and a Ray Goldstein."

"We did have a business dealing recently, but my research showed that it was all on the up-and-up. What seems to be the problem? I'm sure Mr. Goldstein can clear things up for you."

"That's the trouble, Mr. Bradshaw. Mr. Goldstein was found dead in his hotel room last night. What was once a case of fraud has become much more serious. Since you are one of the last people to have been seen with him, the Justice Department needs to speak to you as soon as possible."

18

Gordon put down the phone, stunned. He'd just seen Ray. How could he be dead? He jumped when a hand touched his shoulder.

"You look terrible," said Irena, concern in her eyes. "What happened?"

"Ray Goldstein is dead," he said.

"The man you bought the companies from?"

Gordon managed a weak nod.

"Come get in the car. We'll figure out next steps."

Once back in the passenger seat, Gordon willed himself to take slow, even breaths. Finally, his heart stopped banging against his ribcage. "I'm now a person of interest in Ray's death."

"Is that what they said, death?"

Gordon recalled the conversation. "Yes."

"Well, at least they aren't labeling it a murder," said Irena.

"Yet," said Gordon. "Ray and I have been doing business for several years. I know he liked to live on the edge. He was a pretty hardcore gambler. But this is a shock."

"Maybe he got in bed with the wrong people," said Irena.

Gordon felt like he was in a daze. "I'm supposed to talk to someone at the Department of Justice," he continued. "But if they detain me, you'd be all alone trying to find your father and Sammy."

Irena tried to swallow the lump of emotion that had formed in her throat at Gordon's words. "I'll be okay," she said. "You need to take care of things."

"I have nothing to tell them. The last time I saw Ray, he was very much alive and had unloaded some companies on me. We completed our transaction, and then I paid him well. Afterwards, we did some gambling, and then I met you."

"And I'm such a reliable witness," said Irena wryly.

"There's nothing I can do for Ray now, but I can help you find Sammy and maybe your father. Let's just go find her. I'll sort all of this out later."

Irena studied him for a moment, then replied. "How about we head for Vegas. If you decide to go to the Department of Justice, they probably have an office there."

"That'll work," Gordon agreed.

Irena put the car in drive and headed for the freeway on-ramp going east. "I've been known to get to Vegas from California in five hours," she said. "Hold on."

They arrived in Vegas at midnight, though the bright lights made it seem like daytime.

"It's going to be tough to get into a hotel room without a credit card," said Gordon as they pulled off the freeway.

"I have a solution for that. I found a prepaid credit card in my father's office with a couple thousand on it. That'll cover us."

They decided to check into the Flamingo, next to the Bellagio. After parking the car in the hotel lot and checking in, they went straight to their room.

"Long day." Gordon yawned as the elevator door opened at their floor. He waited for her to exit. Once inside the room, he eyed the king-sized bed and turned to her. "I'd love to stay up and talk with you, but I don't think I would make very good company. I'm really beat."

Irena ran her hand up and down his arm. "No apologies necessary. Sleep well."

Gordon smiled and began undressing as Irena checked out the mini-bar. Opening the small refrigerator, she found a bottle of wine. Pulling it out, she settled into a chair next to the windows overlooking the strip. She twisted the screw top lid and took a long drink, welcoming the feel of the liquid warming her insides. Then her breath caught in her throat as a long-buried memory flashed across her mind.

"Irena, follow my lead. My friend Solana is right behind us. Just do something to cause a distraction."

"But what are we doing, dad?"

"Solana is collecting something due her."

Willing herself not to get red cheeks, Irena walked through the upscale Vegas restaurant, her mind whirring as to how she could cause a distraction. Spying a purse on the back of a woman's chair, she pretended to trip next to the table. As everyone gasped, and a man sprang up to help her, she grabbed the woman's purse and proceeded to run for the front of the restaurant, but the maître de stopped her.

"Give me the purse," he ordered.

Irena pretended not to understand him.

"I said, give me the purse." He reached out and pulled it from her grasp.

A man had come up behind them and grabbed the purse from the maître de. "My wife and I want to prosecute!" he demanded.

"That's our policy, sir," he told the man. "Very sorry for the disturbance. We will comp your meal."

Then the maître de grabbed Irena by the arm and marched her toward the back of the restaurant. She peered around for her father, who she thought would be rescuing her by now, but he was nowhere to be seen.

Everyone in the restaurant watched with disdain in their eyes. Irena felt like crying.

In a back room, the maître de instructed her to sit in a chair. He picked up the phone and called the police, explaining that he'd caught a girl trying to steal a purse. Irena's heart raced in her chest. Was she going to get hauled off to jail?

After he hung up, the maître de put up his hand, as if to stop her from talking. "We don't put up with theft here, no matter how young you are." He began looking at paperwork on his desk, as if Irena didn't exist.

She sat trembling at the terror she felt about going to jail, when a fire alarm sounded. The maître de jumped up. "You stay here!" he ordered, running out of the room.

Irena sprang up and peeked out the doorway into the hall. She spied an exit at the far end of the corridor and raced down the hallway towards freedom. When she passed a door marked office, she heard muffled sounds, then Solana's distinctive voice. Stopping in her tracks, Irena went to the door, which was ajar, peeking inside to see Solana towering over a woman tied to a chair. "Hand over the money, or you'll have a real fire on your hands," Solana warned, then slapped her across the face. Irena's heart skipped a beat when she saw her father reach out and grab Solana's arm. "Calm down, I'm sure she's going to give you your money."

Movement at the other end of the hall reminded Irena about the police coming to get her. She pushed the exit door open and ran into the alley. As police sirens sounded in the distance, she ran until she spotted a diner several blocks away. Inside the restaurant, she headed for the bathroom. Once in a stall, she kneeled in front of the toilet and vomited until there was nothing left in her stomach.

19

Gordon awoke at first light and found Irena sitting at the table staring out the window. He stretched and sat up.

"Did you sleep well?"

Irena didn't respond.

Gordon got out of bed and sat down in the chair across from her. Still staring out the window, she said, "I'm such a fool." She glanced at Gordon. Her eyes registered a sadness he hadn't seen before.

He waited, feeling that if he said anything at all, Irena might shut down. She blinked furiously, but tears came anyway. Gordon found a handful of tissues, then pulled his chair closer to hers. She took the tissues, hiccuping a thank you. Then she dabbed her eyes. "When I said that my father didn't harm anyone?" She hiccuped a sob.

"Yes." Gordon encouraged her.

"I was wrong. I remember an incident with Solana. They had a woman tied up. A restaurant owner."

"They?"

"I saw Solana slapping her around, but my father was there, too. They had me cause a distraction in the dining room while they were tying the woman up and getting money from her. I stole a woman's purse, and then the maître de called the police."

Gordon's heart filled with sadness as he watched Irena relive the scene. He moved closer to her.

"My father would always say we were just have-nots taking from haves," Irena continued. "That we weren't born on the right side of the tracks like some people. But the truth is, we did what we did, and it was wrong."

Gordon reached over and pulled her toward him, encircling her with his arms. "Your father took advantage of your innocence. It's not your fault."

"Why am I just now remembering that incident with Solana? How many more were there?"

"I'm no psychologist, but I'd say that if there were other incidents, you'll remember them when it's time. The mind has a way of protecting itself." He felt Irena's body relax slightly. "C'mon, you're exhausted. Lie down for a few more hours, and you'll feel a lot better."

"Will you lie with me?" she asked, her voice barely a whisper.

Gordon threw the bedspread back and fluffed the pillows as Irena lay down with a heavy sigh. He got in bed and pulled her back against his chest. Stroking her hair, he felt her body slacken and her breathing slow. As she slept, Gordon remained holding her, anger filling him when he thought of Irena as a child, being used by adults in such a way. What else had occurred, he wondered? What was buried so deep in Irena's psyche that she didn't dare uproot those memories?

Irena awoke midday, the sun stealing softly from underneath the curtains, uncertain at first where she was. Then she sensed Gordon beside her, felt his breath soft on her skin. She lay her hand on his chest, reached up to kiss his chin, hoping he would wake, wanting him. Gordon stirred and without speaking pulled her to him. Taking his time, he unbuttoned her blouse, unclasped her bra and kissed her breasts, held them in his hands and rubbed her nipples with his thumbs until they were hard. Irena shimmied her pants down as Gordon got up and stood beside the bed taking off his clothes as Irena watched, her desire heightening.

When he climbed back in bed and the heat of their bodies touched, they held one another, Gordon running his hands down her back, kissing her throat. She felt the beat of his heart against hers. Then he took the fingers of one of her hands and placed them in his mouth. He clenched them gently between his teeth, his mouth warm, tongue circling her fingertips sending ripples of desire through her body. Nuzzling her neck, he whispered soft kisses in her ear, telling her, his lips close, what he wanted to do to her. "You feel so good," he said, running his hand along her legs and squeezing the inside of her thighs, sending ripples of desire throughout her body.

Gordon had never wanted a woman more than Irena. Maybe it was because she was such a mass of contradictions, willing to show him all sides of her. The hardened side that had seen too much, and the little girl who hadn't been sheltered as she should have been. He realized he could love all parts of this woman, and it took him by surprise. He felt slightly dizzy at the realization.

"What do you need? What do you want?" he asked, leaning on one elbow to gaze at her, loving the disheveled way she looked in bed, hair messy, lips swollen and rosy from kissing. He couldn't get over the firm roundness of her bottom, the long lean legs and perfectly flat stomach as his tongue trailed across her skin. But what he loved more than anything was her laughter when she let her raw excitement loose, as if bewildered at the sweet joy between them. Irena obviously loved their sex play, and the more she showed it, the more it flamed Gordon's own passion. Suddenly, he murmured, "I love you." Then he held his breath. But she hadn't heard him. Instead, he made love with her in such a flame of passion, until at last they lay hot and panting beside one another.

When they recovered, Irena turned on her side toward him and smiled. "Let's take a bath together." Again, her silvery laughter filled the room. She hopped out of bed, glancing over her shoulder, Gordon following. Who was this woman, he wondered, aware suddenly of a part of Irena that perhaps neither of them had ever experienced.

Irena turned the faucet on and grabbed some bubble bath, sprinkling a generous amount beneath the running water. A layer of bubbles immediately began to cover the surface.

She looked at him, eyes large and bright with happiness.

"Do you know how beautiful you are?" Gordon ran his fingers in her hair, pulling her face close to his and kissing her.

"Now that sounds like a line," she said, pretending to be angry.

"It's no line, Irena."

With a twist, she turned off the water and tested its temperature. Then she immersed herself beneath a sparkling froth of foam.

Gordon eased into the tub, facing her. She placed one foot on his chest, lowering it to tickle his belly with her toes. He took her foot in his hands. "What do you want me to do with this?"

"A foot rub?" She gave him a wink.

Gordon took a bar of soap, sudsing up her foot, then slowly ran his hand along her legs to the softest part of her. She lay back against the porcelain, the bubbles covering her breasts and closed her eyes, smiling as he caressed her. Suddenly, there sounded a loud knocking on the hotel room door.

"Who could that be?" Gordon sat up in the water.

Irena reached for a towel. "Should we get it?" she whispered.

Gordon climbed out of the tub and wrapped himself in a towel. He indicated with a lift of his chin for her to follow. She scrambled out.

As they neared the door, he put his fingers gently on her lips, his eyes warning her to stay put. Leaning to peer through the peephole, he pulled away, a look of shock on his face. Then he pointed for Irena to take a look. She stepped forward, and in the next instant turned back to him, unable to speak.

"Is that who I think it is?" mouthed Gordon.

Irena felt her knees threaten to buckle. She took hold of the doorknob to steady herself.

"I'll be in the bathroom getting dressed," said Gordon.

Irena opened the door.

"Kezia!"

She couldn't find her voice.

"Are you going to let me in?"

Irena opened the door and motioned him inside. Shutting it, she turned and leaned against it, sure her eyes had created a vision. "Where in the hell have you been for the last three years?" Irena heard herself hiss. "I thought you were dead!"

Her father's eyes wandered around the room. "I've had a rough few days. Have any coffee for your old father?"

"Not until you tell me why I haven't heard from you." Irena's voice was becoming shrill.

"Just let me get a load off, Kezia, and I'll tell you everything."

"My name is Irena."

"Okay, okay. I wasn't sure what alias you were using."

Irena studied her father's face. Though he was trying to act cavalier, she could tell he was spooked.

"Sit down. I'll make you a cup of coffee."

Relief washed over his face. "I knew you'd see things my way…"

"I don't see anything, Dad. Just sit down and try to shut up." Irena took the coffee pot and pulled open the bathroom door to find Gordon standing right behind it.

"Go ahead and introduce yourself, before my father nabs your wallet. I'm going to get dressed and fill the coffee pot with water." She shut the bathroom door.

While she slipped her clothing on and filled the pot with water, Irena heard Gordon say, "Nice to meet you, Mr. Martin. I'm Gordon."

When she came out of the bathroom, her father had taken off his signature black beret that usually covered his bald head and was chatting with Gordon.

"It's very kind of you to let me in," her father said as she walked out with the coffee pot and poured the water into the machine. "I'll just have a bit of coffee and catch up with my daughter. Then I'll get out of your way." Her father sat in one of the chairs, placing his beret on the table in front of him. "May I ask how you two met?"

Irena pushed the brew button on the machine, then stared at her father. Except for the hat, he wore clothing she'd never seen before. The black pants looked foreign cut. The blue shirt, oxford style, which he'd always said was too constraining. When she didn't respond, he looked from Gordon's face to hers. Then understanding filled his eyes. "So, you're working together?"

Irena pulled up a chair across from her father and leaned back in it. "I'm the one who's going to ask questions."

Her father raised his arms and exclaimed, "Go ahead, I'm an open book."

Irena shook her head, willing herself not to let the immense relief and joy she felt at seeing him alive cloud her judgment. There would be time for that once she determined just how much trouble her father was in.

"Where have you been? And I want the truth. The last time I saw you in Poland, I thought you were being kidnapped."

"Oh, that." He sniffed the air. "Is my coffee ready, do you think?"

Irena slammed her palm on the table so hard that her father jumped. Then she stood up and placed both hands on the arms of his chair, leaning close to his face. In a low voice, she said, "I've spent the last three years looking for you. Many people told me you were probably dead, but I kept looking. You are not going to waltz back into my life as if nothing happened." Irena felt her arms shaking as she waited for her father's response. He gaped at her, his blue eyes darting back and forth.

Gordon had heard of the air getting thick with emotion, but he'd never understood the term, until now. So palatable were Irena's emotions —relief mixed with rage—that Gordon felt he needed to do something to relieve the tension. He gently placed his hands on her arms.

"How about we all sit down and talk this through. Give your father a chance to tell you the truth." Gordon removed his hands, and Irena eased back into her chair. He watched as father and daughter eyed one another.

Finally, Walter spoke. "I'm sorry, Irena. I can't explain everything right now. But I did what I did to protect you."

Irena snorted and looked to Gordon. "I told you he could never tell the truth."

Walter sat up in his chair. "You've been talking to him about me?"

"Why the hell not? I thought I'd never see you again."

Walter shifted in his seat uncomfortably. "Look, that last con we did, we were in way over our heads with some very bad people. They did kidnap me. But someone saw to it that I was released."

Irena remained silent, her arms folded across her chest.

Walter fiddled with his beret. "They beat me up pretty good, and I had to go into hiding. If I'd contacted you, you would have become a target. I had to protect you. I know it doesn't look that way, but that's all I've ever tried to do. Protect you."

Irena studied her father's face. He appeared to be genuinely sorry, but then he had spent his life conning people.

She uncrossed her arms. "Have you been taking your medicine?"

Walter reached into his pocket and pulled out two bottles of pills. He shook them. "Yes."

Irena grabbed them from his hand and read the labels. Then she examined the contents. "It looks like Robert O'Brien needs to refill these soon." She slammed them back on the table. "That's a new alias."

"I told you. I had to go deep underground."

Irena shook her head. "How did you find me, anyway?"

"The credit card I left in my room with the tickets to Belize. When I saw you used it last night, I followed the trail."

Irena took a good look at her father. The last three years had given his face a lot of extra lines. She wondered what he'd been doing to get them.

"What now?" she asked. "I know this is more than a family reunion. Tell me, Dad, just how much trouble are you in?"

Walter seemed to weigh his next words as Irena saw a flash of terror skitter across his eyes. "The truth is, I came to warn you that your life is in danger. You need to go off the grid completely."

21

"I'm not going anywhere until you explain everything to me." Irena felt her hackles rising again. It was always the same way with her father. Circular conversations that went nowhere and left her more confused than when they started.

Walter sighed. "It's very complicated. How about that coffee?"

Gordon motioned to stand up, and Irena held up her hand to stop him. "It's always complicated with you, Dad, but fine. I'll get you some damn coffee. Then I want you to answer me."

She went over and poured three cups of coffee and brought them all to the table with the sweeteners. Taking a sip of hers, she set the cup down and waited.

Walter took a few gulps of his coffee, then said, "Someone has a hit out on me, and you could be next."

Irena blew air through her teeth in response.

"Before you dismiss this as all nonsense, hear me out."

"I'm listening," she said, squelching the urge to roll her eyes.

Her father leaned toward her and said in a low voice, "That last con involved the Lithuanian mafia." His eyes searched her face and shock registered in them. "You know about this?"

"Something about it. I told you that I never stopped looking for you."

Walter, stood, knocking his coffee on its side on the table. "I didn't want you involved. I—" Her father was interrupted mid-sentence by a sharp popping sound. Glass from the hotel room window exploded all over the room.

"Gun!" shouted Gordon, who grabbed Irena and pushed her to the floor. Several more shots fired, then the melee stopped. Irena opened her eyes to safety glass on the carpeting. Gordon's arms surrounded her. She squirmed to look at him and asked, "Are you okay?"

"Yes, you?"

"I think so." Irena felt the dry Vegas air filling the room. "My father!" She sprang to sitting and saw Walter unmoving by the table, blood on his chest.

"Dad!" she cried, crawling over to him. "He's been hit."

The hotel room telephone rang, and Gordon crawled over to answer it.

Irena put a finger on her father's neck and felt immense relief wash through her. He had a pulse. Blood seemed to be oozing quickly from his upper chest, though. She ran to grab a towel out of the bathroom and put pressure on the wound to stop the bleeding.

"That was the front desk," said Gordon. "The police and paramedics are on their way up. How's your father?"

"He has a pulse, and it's still pretty strong." She continued to apply pressure to his wound. "Come on, Dad, stay with me," she urged. "You can't go anywhere now that I have you back. I haven't had a chance to tell you how happy I am to see you."

When there was a knock on the hotel room door, Gordon opened it and let two uniformed police officers in. They surveyed the scene. One of the officers went to inspect the window, while the other said, "An off-duty officer saw the shooter on the balcony of the hotel across the way after he made the shots, but he wasn't able to catch him. Can you tell us what happened here?"

"Only what you see," said Gordon. "We were talking at the table. Her father stood up, and shots were fired."

The officer examining the window called out, "I'm going to request CSI."

Just then Irena cried, "His pulse is weakening. Where's the paramedics?"

"Just about here," said the officer speaking to Gordon. "I'm going to need to question you both further, but it's best we vacate this room to do so."

Irena looked up at him, fire in her eyes. "I am not leaving my dad until I know he's on the way to the hospital."

Seconds later, three paramedics rushed into the room and took over with her father. One paramedic, asked, "Has he been unconscious since he was shot?"

"I think so," said Irena. "We all went onto the floor during the shooting."

"Is it possible he hit his head?"

"Yes," said Irena. "Also, he's bipolar. His medication is in his pocket."

The paramedic nodded.

Irena came to stand next to Gordon, who put his arm around Irena and felt her body shaking. He murmured in her ear, "He's still alive."

When the officer began questioning them again, Irena interrupted. "I want to go to the hospital with my father."

"Someone tried to shoot one or all of you, Miss. What's your name? I have more questions."

"Irena Martin," she said, as the paramedics began to wheel Walter out of the room on a stretcher. "Where are you taking him?" she called out.

"Kindred Hospital," answered one. "Are you family?"

"Yes."

"Go to the emergency room. They'll give you updates as they come in." He turned and rushed out of the room.

"I need your contact information, Miss Martin, and then you can go." The officer stood with his pen poised over a notepad.

Gordon addressed the officer. "I'm sorry, she's understandably very upset." He gave him their burner phone number as Irena went to pick up her bag. The officer interrupted her. "You'll have to leave your belongings here for CSI."

Just then, the CSI crew entered, and the officer went to speak to them as Irena tucked her bag under her arm and handed Gordon his. He pulled the cellphone charger from the wall and stuffed it in his pocket. Then they quickly left the room.

"This way," said Irena, pointing to a doorway marked stairs. She turned the knob and stepped inside the stairwell. Gordon followed. As she started down the stairs, he called out, "Wait."

She turned to him.

"I think you know what I'm going to say," he said quietly.

Irena sighed. "That it's not safe for me to go see my father in the hospital?" He watched as her chin trembled slightly. "All that time, I hoped. Prayed even. And now I might lose him again."

Gordon reached out and embraced her. "He's going to be fine."

After a moment, Irena pulled back and gazed into his eyes. "You're right. He's strong. Always has been. I still don't understand why you're helping me, but I'm grateful."

"I must be terrible at giving signals," said Gordon, who was about to tell her how he felt when the phone in Irena's purse buzzed.

"I guess the phone got turned on rolling around in my bag," she said, pulling the phone out and eyeing it warily.

Gordon saw the text on the screen. *Next time, I won't miss. They might save your father in ER, but he isn't going to make it out of the hospital alive.*

22

At seeing the fear in Irena's eyes, Gordon willed himself to focus so he could assure her. "I'm going to call my contact at the NSA and get the name of a private security firm to protect your father."

Irena nodded gratefully as Gordon made the call.

"Gordon, for Christ's sake. Where the hell are you?" asked his friend Benson when he answered.

"I can't say, but I need your help," said Gordon.

"Did you talk to the SEC?"

"I talked to them, but I haven't gone in yet. I have bigger problems than that."

"How in the hell could you have bigger problems than that?"

Gordon hesitated.

"Miss AKA? Did you know she has a redacted record?"

That news caused Gordon pause. "No, when?"

"When she was a kid. Look, Gordon, I get it. I've seen her photo. She's a knockout. But it's time to take care of yourself."

Gordon glanced at Irena, who studied his face as he spoke.

"Forget I called."

"Wait! Shit. You and I go way back, and I owe you. What kind of help do you need?" said Benson.

Gordon told him about Irena's father needing protection at the hospital.

"Okay, I'll get a call out immediately to a high-level security firm we contract with and put it on your tab. What else?"

"Can you get me information on a Solana Petrauskas? Background, known associates and where she might be?"

"Okay, I'll get back to you on what I dig up. Anything else?"

Gordon chuckled. "If you can keep the SEC at bay, that'd be perfect."

"Sorry, no contacts there. I've heard they're real hard asses, by the way."

Once he hung up, Irena asked, "What's our next move?"

"We need somewhere to hole up that's not our hotel room."

The burner phone sounded then, and Gordon checked the screen. "It's Tony." He answered.

"You two can't seem to stay out of trouble."

"I take it you heard," said Gordon.

"Tell me that right before you were shot at you got some information on Sammy's whereabouts."

"I'm afraid not," said Gordon.

"Listen, I know you're both motivated, but let the professionals take over from here. I've got agents coming into town within the hour to question Irena's father after he's out of surgery, if he pulls through. Let me give you the address of a safehouse on the outskirts of Vegas. Go there and lay low for now."

When Gordon got off the phone, he told her what Tony said, but Irena felt uneasy. There was something he wasn't telling her, but she couldn't figure out what. Downstairs, they slipped through the crowded lobby, filled with anxious guests, media and law enforcement. Out front, they caught a cab to the safehouse.

"You're quiet," said Irena, studying Gordon's profile as he looked out the window at the Vegas streets.

"Just thinking about next steps."

Irena scooted closer to him. "I can help. What is it? The SEC?"

"Let's talk about it when we get to the house." Gordon resumed looking out the window, leaving Irena feeling confused and all alone. Those were feelings she hated more than anything.

"We'll have a warm bed for the next few nights, Irena, if you do exactly what I say. And I can buy you that doll you saw on television. The one with the pink dress and bows."

Irena clung to her father's hand. "Please, Dad, I don't want you to leave me here."

"I always come back for you, don't I? I'll see you really soon. I showed you how to use the lighter, remember? Watch the clock and light the drapes when it says three, and I'll meet you in the parking lot. Just climb out the window and down the fire escape like we practiced."

"What if I fall?"

"I'll be right there to catch you."

"But, Dad, why do I have to do this?"

"Just do what I said, and we'll go get your doll, okay?" Her father left the hotel room, and Irena stood there shaking, her eyes glued to the clock, which read 2:50.

Irena sat up, peering around the taxicab, the memory still lingering in her head.

"What is it?" Gordon asked.

"I don't know. I don't feel well." Her stomach swirled.

"Do you need the driver to pull over?"

Irena took some deep breaths. "I'll be alright. Are we almost there?"

"About ten minutes," called out the driver.

Irena sat back in her seat, searching the corners of her mind for more pieces of the memory. Where had she been? What had she done with the lighter? The thought made her feel uncomfortable. She had been about six, she thought, and she remembered the doll. She had carried it everywhere. Irena glanced at Gordon, but he was still peering out the window.

When they arrived at a one-story house in a suburban cul-de-sac, the key was right where Tony told them it would be. They went inside. The living room contained wooden furniture decorated with blue and red Native American blankets and pillows. The shades were down, and a clock ticked on the wall.

She set her purse on a couch and turned to Gordon. "Are you going to tell me what's eating you?"

He regarded her for a moment, as if she were a business adversary, and Irena's stomach dropped. She knew this was all too good to last. "If you're sorry that you got mixed up in all of this and want to opt out, I understand," she told him.

Gordon stepped closer, pulling her chin up slightly so she would meet his eyes. "Has any of this been real?"

Irena blinked. "What?"

"Has any of this been genuine?"

"I don't understand. Did your friend say something about me to you on the phone?"

Gordon was silent.

"You might as well tell me before you leave," she said, pulling away from him and stepping back.

"Why didn't you tell me you have a redacted record as a child?"

"What are you talking about?"

"You were taken into custody at some point as a child."

Visions of smoke and fire engines flashed before Irena's eyes. Her stomach roiled.

23

Gordon held Irena's hair back as she vomited in the bathroom toilet. He could tell by the look on her face when he mentioned her redacted record that she had perhaps been too young to remember. After she washed her face with cold water, they made their way to the living room. Irena sat down, and Gordon went to the kitchen and poured her some water.

"I'm sorry if you didn't remember," he said as he handed her the glass.

Irena took a small sip and set the water down on the coffee table. "Most people would probably know if they had been taken to jail as a child. But the way I grew up. There have always been fuzzy spots in my memory about my childhood. I just figured my mind was protecting me. But I never imagined..."

Gordon felt terrible about the conversation he'd started. "Maybe it's better left not remembered. I shouldn't have said anything."

"You got the information from your friend at the NSA? Did he say how old I was?"

"No, just that you were a child." Listening to his own words, Gordon realized how childish his accusing her had been. But then caring for a woman like this was all new terrain for him.

Irena was silent for what seemed like a long time. When she finally spoke, her voice was quiet. "I meant what I said. If you want to leave to take care of your own stuff, I totally understand."

"I'm not going anywhere," said Gordon, moving closer. "We'll figure all of this out, and then I can deal with the SEC."

"I'll pay you back somehow for all that you've done for me. I promise." She looked at him with such earnestness that Gordon's heart clutched. He reached over and pulled her toward him, noticing how she fit perfectly against his chest, his chin resting on her head. They sat that way for a time as the daylight waned, neither speaking.

When Irena felt Gordon fall asleep, she slid out of his embrace and eased him back onto the couch, propping a pillow under his head. He murmured when she did so, and she smiled and lightly kissed his lips. She knew he felt badly about bringing up her record, but she was glad he said something. She'd always wondered about the bits and pieces that would come to her at times that made no sense. Now another big piece of the puzzle had been put into place.

She took the burner phone Gordon had set on the table into the kitchen, looked up the emergency room number and dialed. When the operator came on the line, she said, "I'm checking on the condition of a patient. His name is Walter Martin. I'm his daughter."

After long minutes ticked by, the operator returned and connected her with the nurse's station. A nurse came on the line. "Your father is in surgery to remove two bullets."

"Did he regain consciousness, do you know?"

"From what I can tell, no, he hasn't. The surgery should be completed within the next couple of hours, if you'd like to check back."

Irena thanked her and hung up. Glancing at the cupboards, she wondered if they contained anything decent to make for dinner. She located a meal prep kit and frozen ground beef and got to work.

Anything to keep her mind off something going wrong with the surgery.

When Gordon awoke, the living room was dark, but the kitchen light shone bright. His stomach growled at the smell of food. He found Irena at the stove and put his arms around her from behind. "I thought you didn't cook? Smells delicious."

She laughed and pointed with a spatula to a box on the counter. "I can follow directions. It'll be ready in a minute."

"I'm starving," he said, kissing the side of her neck.

"How about setting the table."

"I can do that." Gordon reluctantly pulled away and took plates out of the cupboard and silverware from a drawer.

"There's something I want to tell you. But let's eat first," she said, a serious tone to her voice.

When they sat down with their plates full, Gordon said, "Thank you."

"You might want to wait before saying that." Irena picked up her fork, took a bite and smiled. "This is actually pretty good."

They ate in silence for a time. Once her plate was clear, Irena pushed it away and put her elbows on the table. "When you were sleeping, I was thinking about my past and memories that I never understood."

Gordon lowered his fork. "And?"

"I might know where Solana is holding Sammy. There was this cabin out in the Sonoran Desert. We went there sometimes. My father told me it was Solana's vacation home. I always thought that was odd, because it had very little furniture and was often filled with boxes that she'd tell me not to touch. I really felt uncomfortable when I was there."

"Any idea where the cabin is?" Gordon reached over and took her hand.

"No, but my father does. I called the hospital while you were asleep.

He was still in surgery." Irena pushed her glass of water around on the table with the hand Gordon wasn't holding. "I know he'll come out of this. He always does." She stopped moving the glass. "You know, I always looked up to my father. Hung on his every word. He had such a way of making each of our cons an adventure. And I thought that's the way everyone lived. When I got older, I realized I was different. The other kids didn't live in hotel rooms." She laughed and took a drink of water, then continued.

"The worst was finally realizing that my father was never going to change. I was so mad at him the night he disappeared three years ago. For the first few days, I was glad he was gone. Until I realized that he wasn't coming back. I thought when he showed up at our hotel room this morning, I'd finally be able to get some answers."

"Like you just said, your father is going to pull through, and you'll get your answers. My friend came through on the security agency. They're watching over him now."

"That's a huge relief. Thank you. I'm going to see if he's out of surgery." As Gordon cleaned up the kitchen, Irena waited for the operator to connect her with the nursing station. After a good five minutes, a nurse came on the line.

"Good news, Miss Martin, your father made it out of surgery with flying colors. He's still under heavy sedation, but we expect him to be awake in a few hours, although too groggy to talk. I would call in the morning."

When Irena shut the speaker phone off to end the call, Gordon said, "Sounds like he'll be alert enough to tell us the location of the cabin."

Irena nodded and thought how she also wanted to know why he left her in a motel room with a lighter when she was six years old.

24

"We're going to need the car we left in the hotel parking lot," said Gordon the next morning as they traveled back to Vegas in a cab.

"And new clothes to disguise ourselves before going into the hospital," Irena said. "There's a mall near the hotel."

"I don't think you should go in to see your father," said Gordon. "It could be dangerous. They'll be expecting you. I'll go instead."

Irena frowned at Gordon's words, then nodded. "Okay. Maybe our best bet is making you look like hired security." She recalled the many times she had dressed herself and her father for cons.

When they entered a small clothing shop for men, a woman greeted them. "Let me know if you need any assistance," she called out to them.

"Do you want help?" Irena whispered to Gordon.

"I think you should dress me," he said.

Irena found a couple of charcoal gray suits and several light gray dress shirts. She handed them to Gordon, who headed for the dressing room. It didn't take long to find an outfit that made him look official. While Gordon paid for the suit with cash, Irena went out front of the store to call the hospital and check on her father's condition.

"My dad is awake," she told him when he came out, dressed in his new clothing. "I'll stay here out front of this store while you go."

"I'll get back here as soon as possible," he said.

"Promise?" Irena found herself blurting out. She reddened. "I mean, okay."

Gordon smiled. "I promise."

As Gordon walked away, Irena found her pulse quickening and then racing. An all too familiar feeling that she hadn't had in a long time.

"I'm done with you, Dad! Done with all of this. If you leave right now, I'm never going to talk to you again."

"Don't be so dramatic, Irena. I'll be back in a couple of days."

"Have you taken your medicine, Dad?"

"No, I haven't taken my damn medicine. I don't need it anymore."

"Yes, you do!"

"She says I don't."

"Who?"

"Just sit tight. I'll be back soon."

Feeling frustrated and alone, Irena watched as her father walked out the front door.

When Gordon arrived at the hospital, he headed for Recovery. He smiled at the nurse on duty as he pointed to a set of double doors, announcing, "I'm part of the team watching over your patient, Walter Martin."

The woman glanced at his attire and smiled. "Go ahead in." She pushed a button, causing the doors to swing open as she answered a ringing phone.

In the Recovery unit, Gordon scanned the hallway. At the end of the corridor stood a man in a suit. Striding toward him with purpose, Gordon gave the guard a half smile.

The man viewed him suspiciously. "Who are you?"

"Family lawyer. He knows me."

"I'll check with him. You stay out here."

Gordon nodded as the guard went to talk to Walter. When Irena's father glanced at the doorway and saw Gordon, he recognized him, and the guard waved him over.

Walter was hooked up to several monitors and IVs, but otherwise looked good. He started to sit up, but Gordon put out his hand to stop him.

"Better not to strain yourself."

Walter laid back on his pillow. "Where's Irena? Is she okay?"

"She's safe. But we need your help to keep her that way." Gordon got close, speaking in a low voice. "We need to find Solana and stop her."

Walter started to protest. "I tried to keep Irena out of all of this. There are things it's best she never knows."

"Well, now she's in the thick of it."

Walter looked genuinely distressed. "What can I do to help?"

"Give me the location of Solana's cabin in the Sonoran Desert."

Walter's eyes widened. "You can't go there."

Gordon took a deep breath. "I don't want to play hardball with you, but if I have to, I will. Give me the location, or the men guarding you will disappear."

Walter studied Gordon's face. "Solana is dangerous, but she'd never hurt Irena. I can't promise that her associates won't, though. That's one reason I've tried to keep her out of this."

"A young woman and her baby's life are also at stake. We need the location."

"If I give it to you, will you promise to take care of my little girl?"

"I give you my word."

On his way back to Irena a few minutes later, Gordon placed an overdue phone call.

"Hi, Mom, how's your day going?"

"Rex, it's so nice to hear from you. Is all okay? I've been trying to call you, but your phone keeps going straight to voicemail."

"My phone is on the fritz, so I've got a temporary one. What did you call about?"

"Your dad was wanting to talk to you. He keeps asking when he'll see you again to play checkers. I told him you were busy but would see him soon."

"I'll get there as soon as I can. I'm in the middle of something right now."

"I can tell by the tone of your voice. Another big business deal?"

Irena flashed through Gordon's mind. "Something like that."

"Promise me you'll take some time to relax once you're done, honey."

"I promise, Mom. And I'll see you and Dad soon."

When Gordon walked into the mall a few minutes later, he was relieved to see Irena standing in front of the store where he'd left her. As he approached, she smiled, then ran to embrace him. Squeezing him tight, she exclaimed, "You came right back."

Of course, he came right back, Gordon thought, as he held Irena. He'd become one of those men he always joked about. Hopelessly in love with a woman and willing to do anything for her.

25

"You have a funny look on your face. What did my father say?"

"He gave me the address. And he said, I quote, 'Take care of my little girl.' "

Irena smiled. "I'm glad he's okay. Thank you again for the guards. I meant it when I said I would pay you back some—."

Gordon cut her off with a slow and deep kiss. When he finished, he said, "There, now you've paid me back. Not another word about it."

Irena struggled to find an answer, but nothing came to mind.

"Let's order some coffee and do a map search for Solana's cabin, so we can get the lay of the land," he said.

"Should we tell Tony?"

Gordon set his laptop on a bistro table. "Good idea."

Irena dialed Tony's number as she sat down. "Straight to voicemail. Should we check in with Twitch?"

"I'd hate to give him false hope, but he might have some information for us."

Twitch answered before the first ring completed. "Sammy?"

"Sorry, Twitch, it's Irena. But we have a lead on where she might be. We're headed there soon. Is Tony around?"

"Didn't he talk to you? He also had a lead. He left last night."

"Where did he go?"

"I don't know. He told me to wait here in case she calls back."

"Stay strong, Twitch," said Irena. "We're going to find her." She hoped that was true.

"Not much out where Solana's cabin is, but that's no surprise," said Gordon. He turned the computer toward Irena so she could see the satellite image of the property. At the view of the low-slung shack, Irena felt a heavy sense of dread. "I'm going to get a pastry," she said suddenly. "Do you want anything?"

Gordon gave her a meaningful look. "Besides you?"

She laughed, which dispelled some of the tension in her stomach. "Yes, besides me."

"Coffee and pastry would be great."

As Irena stood in line to order, she felt a warm rush of pleasure at Gordon's words. Was it possible he had feelings for her beyond enjoying her body? She snuck a glance behind her, then feeling silly, she turned back and stared straight ahead. Irena had learned the hard way that wanting something too much always ended in disaster.

"Dad, please. I'm asking you to act like a normal father for just one night."

"No worries, Irena. I'm going to bake cookies for your slumber party, and if you want, I can tell a ghost story."

"Dad, I'm sixteen. We talk about boys, not ghosts. Just leave us be."

"If you want me to leave you be, why are you so worried about what I'll do?"

"Just come and check on us sometimes, and act normal, okay? The girls should be here soon, so make yourself scarce."

Irena had taken time getting ready for her birthday party. She had deep cleaned the house and decorated the living room with sky-blue balloons and crepe paper. There was probably way too much food—snacks filled the coffee table—but she wanted to make sure that the three girls she invited had their favorites.

When the hour arrived and no one came, Irena began to pace. An hour later, she called the girls. Two answered with lame excuses, and one call went to voicemail.

As she held back tears and started to throw away the food, there was a knock on the door.

"Hermann. What are you doing here?"

"I heard there was a birthday party." He looked at all the food on the coffee table. "Yum!" Walking in, he reached down for a tortilla strip, sticking it in the guacamole. "My favorite."

"Did my dad call you?"

"Don't get mad at him. He just wants you to have a good birthday. Hermann's here, so now you will! We can even talk about boys." He winked at her, and Irena couldn't help but laugh.

They took the coffees and pastries Irena bought with them while they retrieved the old car from the Flamingo parking lot. After filling it up with gas, they headed south toward the Sonoran Desert.

"It's going to take us nearly seven hours to get there, so get comfortable," said Gordon.

"The radio in this old clunker doesn't work," noted Irena. "How about you tell me more about you. What did you like to do as a kid?"

"The typical sports," Gordon said, steering the car onto the highway, "but I also enjoyed making money. When I was eleven, I started a lawn mowing business. I talked the neighborhood into trying out my services for a month. After that, everyone signed on as a customer. Things were going great, but after the first summer, I realized I hated cutting lawns."

Irena laughed. "Did you quit?"

"Not exactly. I knew the business was worth something—I had a dozen clients on weekly contracts—so I had my sister run things, and I got a cut. She kept it going for years."

"Your sister, Angela, the liberal?"

Gordon chuckled. "Turns out she was a tree-hugger, too, so it was a perfect fit."

"I always wondered what it would be like to have a real family."

"I know she died when you were very young, but do you remember your mother at all?"

"No, and, believe me, I've tried."

"Your father must have shown you photos."

"He told me there are none, but I never really believed him. More likely he threw them away when he was having a depressive episode."

When the cabin came into view, it was sunset. Gordon pulled to the side of the road and stopped the car.

Irena looked out at the desert terrain. Saguaro cactus cast shadows as the coral-colored sky dimmed. Any other time, the beautiful scene would have calmed Irena, but she felt her gut clench and her heart rate pick up speed.

"Maybe we shouldn't do this," she said. "You...we could get killed."

"Let's just go in on foot from here and check things out from a distance. We can see if it looks like the cabin is occupied. If so, we can come back to the car and try calling Tony again."

Irena nodded. "That sounds like a good idea. Let's go before the sun sets and we can't see anything." They got out of the car, and she tried to steady her nerves. All she had to do was pretend this was a con and focus on the task at hand. Get in and get out.

As they got closer to the cabin, Irena's breathing became shallower. Visions of another time flashed in front of her eyes, but she couldn't make sense of them. Or the bits and pieces of words she heard in another language. What had happened in this place to make Irena feel as if a hornet's nest had been let loose in her head? Gordon must have sensed her unease, because he reached out to take her hand.

26

In retrospect, Irena could see that she should have stopped and waited until the memories had subsided. She was distracted by them, and Gordon was distracted by her. That was no match for Solana's guard, who came up behind them and stuck a rifle in Gordon's back.

"Stop moving."

"We're here to see Solana," said Irena. "Let her know Irena is here."

The guard called someone on his phone and spoke in Lithuanian. Then before Irena knew what was happening, he hit Gordon on the side of the head with the rifle, knocking him out.

"What are you doing?" Irena yelled. She tried to go to Gordon, but the guard grabbed her with one arm and hauled her toward the cabin. When they were several feet away, the cabin door slammed open. Solana stalked onto the porch and put her hands on her hips.

"Irena, I see you got my many messages."

The guard let go of her, and she looked back from where they'd come, peering into the quickly dimming light to see if Gordon had regained consciousness.

"Aronas hits hard. Your friend will be out for a while."

"What do you mean, I got your messages?" Irena moved towards the cabin, glancing behind Solana. The interior of the cabin was dark. She couldn't make anything out.

"You're looking for the computer hacker in the cabin."

"Yes. Give Sammy to me, and I'll leave."

Solana looked up at the sky, as if imploring the gods for patience. "We have some business, you and I. Sammy, as you call her, was instrumental in my plan. As was your father."

"Leave Dad out of this."

Solana laughed, a grating sound. "Your father is right in the middle of this, as always. This time with bullets in his chest. I know he wants to protect you, but it's high time you understood what's really going on."

When Gordon awoke, his head pounded, and his hands and feet were bound. He lay on the floor in what must be the cabin. He heard a moan coming from a few feet away. Struggling to focus his eyes in the dark room, lit only by weak moonlight coming through the windows, he made out a woman lying nearby.

"Irena?" he whispered. "Is that you?"

"No, my name is Sammy. Who are you?"

"Gordon. I—we, came to get you. Do you know what happened to the woman I came with?"

"They took her away."

"Where?"

"I don't know. Did Twitch send you?"

"Yes, in a roundabout way. Irena, the woman they took, you hacked her computer."

"Something I will regret for the rest of my life, if I have one," said Sammy.

"Where are you taking me?" Irena asked as they headed away from the cabin. Solana sat in the front passenger seat of a sedan driven by Aronas, and she was in the back. Irena was worried about Gordon. Before they left, he was still unconscious when Solana's guard threw him in the cabin and bound him. Irena had tried to get Sammy's attention, but the girl wouldn't make eye contact.

"I'm taking you to our compound."

"What was that we just left?"

Solana waved her hand. "That shack is just a waystation, as the Americans say. A place to transfer our shipments."

"Yes, that's what we Americans say," said Irena.

Solana turned to glare at her from the front seat. "You aren't American."

"What the hell are you talking about?"

Solana snorted and turned around to face the road, muttering under her breath.

"I've got money," Irena continued, "if that's what you want."

"I know. I cleaned out your account. How do you think I got your attention?"

"I've got a lot more in an offshore account."

"I have plenty of my own money."

"Then what more do you want from me?" Irena asked.

Solana reached into the glove compartment and extracted a box of cigarettes. She lit one.

"Can I have one?" asked Irena, thinking maybe she needed a new strategy for befriending Solana.

Leaning back in her seat, Solana blew out several fat smoke rings. "No, they are bad for your health."

Before long, they came to a tall, metal gate flanked by large mesquite trees. Once it opened, Aronas headed the car down a flagstone road lit by floodlights. They came to a stop in the middle of a circular drive in front of a Mediterranean-style villa. In the bright artificial light, Irena saw a portico entryway and a second-floor deck with bougainvillea spilling over a railing.

"Here we are," said Solana, who got out of the car and instructed Irena to do the same. She lifted her arms as if to present the house to Irena. "Thirteen bedrooms, an indoor and outdoor pool, a grand dining room, though we've never used it. Perhaps we will now, to celebrate your homecoming."

Irena stood gaping at the house. Homecoming?

"I know, my dear, this will take some getting used to. It's many steps up from those ratty motel rooms that Walter drug you to."

Irena didn't know what to make of Solana's cryptic innuendos. Right now, she was more concerned about Gordon.

"What about my friend?"

Solana looked at her blankly.

"The man you left in the shack?"

Solana let out a short laugh that sounded like a bark. "Your paramour? I admit he is quite attractive, but he doesn't fit in this situation. Neither does that rag doll. I'm going to have them disposed of tonight."

Irena knew that reacting to Solana's comment could likely make her explosive. Instead, Irena asked, "Can we go inside?"

"Of course! Excuse my bad manners." They walked up a handful of steps and Solana pushed open heavy oak double doors and stepped into a foyer. "The skylight lights up this room in the daytime," said Solana, pointing above them. "Let me show you the rest of the house."

The tour took a good twenty minutes, the last part finding them below ground in a subterranean spa with a large lap pool, sauna, hot tub and indoor tennis courts.

"I do love tennis," said Solana, "but it's much too hot here to play outdoors. Do you play?"

Irena shook her head. "Not many tennis courts in motels." She didn't know how to get the woman back on track with the urgent matter of Gordon and Sammy.

Solana spread her arms wide as if she might take flight. "It's time for you to take your place in the family business. Your father gave you basic training. Now I'll take over, so you can one day run this empire."

"And what if I don't want to?"

"As my daughter, it's your obligation."

27

Irena stared at Solana. "My mother died in a car accident when I was two," she stammered.

"Just a story your father made up, so you wouldn't have questions about me."

The confusion and horror overtaking Irena had her breathless. How was this possible? So many times, she had imagined her mother being soft and gentle and kind. Nothing like this woman.

Solana came closer to Irena. "No more insipid cons for my Irena. I always told your father you were too good for that."

"If you're looking for reconciliation, that's not going to happen," said Irena, stepping back.

Solana threw back her head and laughed a harsh, dry sound. "Such a sense of humor. So American. Though I must admit that's what attracted me to your father. And his gift for graft." Solana's eyes narrowed as she studied Irena's face. "But your father was always too weak for all of this. And you aren't. I can see you in me."

"I'll never be like you," said Irena.

"You're more like me than you think. The fire. When you were six. A man died."

Fragments of memory hit Irena, filling her nostrils with smoke. It wasn't her father who had given her the lighter and left her in the motel room, it was Solana. She instructed Irena on how the best way to get a fire going quickly is to light the drapes. Solana had threatened to hurt her father if Irena didn't start the fire.

Anger overcame Irena. She advanced on her mother, pushing her hard and yelling, "How could you? I was only six!"

Solana fell back and crashed into the pool, then surfaced, sputtering and pushing her hair out of her face. "And you say you're nothing like me. I gave you a lighter that night, and you did just as I said." Mascara ran down her face, making Solana look even more crazy than she sounded.

"Where was my father?"

"I had to restrain him that night. He wouldn't play along. He never did. That's why I kidnapped him three years ago and had him shot yesterday. He would be dead if I wanted him to be, by the way."

Irena's memories swirled in her head as she ran out of the spa and up the stairs to the living room. Just as she reached the front door, a large arm grabbed her by the hair, pulling her back. Aronas. Solana soon emerged, wrapped in a robe, her hair dripping.

"Bring her into the front bedroom," she instructed him.

Irena tried to struggle, but the giant man's muscles held her tight as he effortlessly brought her to a bedroom and threw her on the bed. Irena's eyes searched for an escape as the man stood over her. Then to her horror, Solana took out a needle from a bureau and filled the syringe from a bottle.

"What the hell is that?"

"Something to calm you down."

Irena sat up and put her arms behind her back. "I won't try to leave. Just don't give me that." She couldn't let them knock her out. She had to get back to Gordon before Solana did.

"I don't believe you," said Solana, motioning for Aronas to restrain Irena. As he held her down tight, Solana stuck the needle in her upper arm. Irena felt herself drifting into blackness.

"How long do they usually stay away?" asked Gordon, who had managed to push himself over to an old chair and was rubbing the ropes that held his hands together against a splintered section of wood.

"It varies."

Gordon loosened the ropes around his hands enough to release them. Then he untied his feet. He was undoing Sammy's hands when a car pulled up.

"Follow my lead," he whispered, then took up his prior place, pretending to be bound.

The guard came in, smacking the door against the wall and advancing towards Gordon. When he reached down, Gordon rushed his legs, taking the man by surprise and sending him thudding onto the floor. Gordon quickly grabbed the chair and walloped him across the head several times until he fell back and passed out.

"His car keys," said Sammy.

Gordon searched the man's pockets and pulled out a set of keys and his cellphone. He reached behind him and yanked a gun from his waist band. Then he grabbed the ties that had bound Sammy and secured the man's hands and feet. "That'll give us some time."

They climbed into the truck in front of the cabin, and Gordon stopped to catch his breath and think. Then he handed the cellphone to Sammy. "Call Twitch. He'll want to know you're okay."

Sammy dialed the number. "It's me. Yes, Gordon found me. We're not in the clear yet, but I'm on my way back to you." There was a pause as Sammy listened to the news Gordon figured Twitch couldn't wait any longer to tell her. Sammy's eyes widened and tears sprang to them. "A baby. Oh, I hoped it was true! Yes, I'm okay. I'm coming home Twitch. I love you, too."

She was about to power the phone off, when Gordon said, "Wait.

Check the phone's geolocator to see where the guard has been recently. That may be where they're holding Irena."

Sammy started to press buttons on the phone, then stopped. "Wait, I'm pregnant. I have to think of the baby. I need you to take me home right now."

"I can't leave Irena."

"Well, then we've got a problem."

Just then a car approached the cabin driving full speed toward them. "Shit." Gordon put the car into gear to back up and turned the truck around. "Get down!" he cried as he floored it and sped past the car. Then without any idea which way to go, he headed north.

28

"How about a compromise?" Gordon spoke over the roar of the truck as he barreled down the road. "Give me Irena's location. Then we check you into a motel. You can call Twitch and have him come get you. If he drives through the night, he'll be here by early morning."

Sammy looked thoughtful, then began working on the phone. Gordon took it as a yes. "The WIFI is spotty, but I think I got the coordinates. I'll put them into the GPS." As she did so, an address popped up.

"We should also check in with Tony," Gordon added.

Sammy nodded. "Fortunately, I have a photographic memory when it comes to phone numbers," she said as she punched in his number. "Tony. I'm with Gordon and okay, but I don't know for how long. Where are you?"

She listened, her eyebrows raising. "Okay, I'll keep you posted."

Gordon looked to Sammy.

"He's in Lithuania. He got a tip that led him to a compound where Solana has a huge weapons arsenal. The Lithuanian police just raided it a few minutes ago."

Gordon's mind flew over their options, but none of them were good. He glanced at the truck's gas gauge. Less than a quarter full. His stomach clenched when he thought of Irena. What was Solana doing

114

with her? The GPS showed that he was heading away from her location.

Relief poured through him when he saw a motel sign with a flashing vacancy light. Gordon exited the freeway and headed for the parking lot. He handed Sammy the remaining cash in his pocket.

"Thanks for agreeing to this," he said.

She gave him the phone. "I would avoid turning this back on. I'll call Twitch from the hotel phone. Be careful and good luck."

Irena struggled to pull herself out of a cottony haze. She blinked at the blurry vision of a bedpost. As she attempted to sit up in bed, she heard shrieking. The door to the room flew open, and Solana strode in. "My compound in Lithuania has been raided! This changes everything."

Irena struggled to focus on Solana's face.

"Aronas, bring the drink."

Irena watched with trepidation as Solana's right-hand man came into the room with a glass of liquid.

"What's that?" she struggled to say.

"Something to wake you up, so you can be of use."

Irena shut her mouth tight as Aronas descended on her. He reached around the back of her head and forced the drink to her mouth. Reluctantly, she took a sip. To her relief, within mere seconds, the beverage did sharpen her senses.

Her mother nodded in approval. "Good." She handed Irena a laptop. "Now transfer the funds in your offshore account into mine. I've got my offshore account up on the screen."

Irena stared at the computer.

"I have a man standing next to your father's hospital bed right now." She held up her cellphone. "All I have to do is say the word."

"How do I know you won't say the word, anyway."

Gordon headed toward the address on the GPS, hoping Irena was there. Now that he had the guard's gun, he tried to recall what Benson had taught him about shooting the few times they'd gone to the gun range together.

When he neared the destination and saw lights in the distance, the truck began sputtering. Taking his foot off the gas, he let the vehicle coast, all the while cursing his stupidity for not filling the tank. The car then made a sudden shudder as he pulled to the side of the road and turned off the engine. Grabbing the gun from the glovebox, he got out and started walking.

"I am losing my patience with you." Solana's agitation level was rising. "It's time for me to get out of town, and I need those funds transferred."

Irena knew that she had the upper hand here. Without the money, mommy dearest wasn't going anywhere. "I need assurances that you won't harm my father."

"Fine! I'll call my man and tell him to stand down."

Irena crossed her arms over her chest. "And I want you to give me the locations of your other stash sites. I know there's one in Poland."

Surprise flashed across Solana's face.

"My guess is there's at least three more locations," Irena continued, seeing she'd hit a nerve.

Solana smiled then. "I told you we are alike. We could have made a good team."

"Give me the locations; I'll transfer the funds. If anything happens to my father, or anyone else I care about, I'm going to the authorities."

She watched Solana do a quick calculation. "Are you referring to your lover? Or your friend Hermann?"

"They don't deserve your wrath."

Solana shook her head. "No man tries to help any woman. They always want something. But in good faith, I'll call my man and tell him not to kill your lover, if he hasn't done so already."

Irena's heart thudded as her mother dialed her phone.

Soon, Solana began yelling in Lithuanian. She threw the phone across the room. "It seems our captives have escaped."

29

Gordon arrived at the front gate of the compound and checked the perimeter with the cellphone flashlight. A fence surrounded the property. The gate had concrete end posts with ridges on them, allowing him to scale one and climb down the other side. Spotting a camera on the gate, he ran quickly down the drive, hoping not to be spotted.

When he neared the house, Gordon crouched and caught his breath. He heard distant voices and wondered how many guards were on watch. He had to throw them off-kilter. He ran along the right side of the compound toward the back, scanning the side of the structure in the dim moonlight. Locating what looked like a power box, he opened the lid and shined the cellphone flashlight inside, locating the main switch. When he flipped it off, the property plunged into darkness.

Gordon heard shouts immediately. Taking advantage of the chaos and confusion, he moved quickly to the back door. It was unlocked. Opening the door as quietly as possible, he slid inside and stopped to let his eyes adjust. He soon focused on a hulking refrigerator and gleaming marble kitchen island. Gun drawn, he tiptoed toward the sound of voices.

"Aronas, check the power box," said Solana. She pointed to Irena. "Keep doing that transfer."

"I can't without power," said Irena. "It knocked the WIFI off." Irena turned the laptop to her mother.

"Aronas, hurry," Solana cried over her shoulder.

Just then, the sound of struggling erupted in the house. Irena jumped when a gun fired.

Solana rushed across the room and pulled a gun out of a bureau. It glinted in the dim light. "Stay here," she ordered, then peered out the doorway and made her way into the hallway.

Irena's mind struggled to figure out what to do. Had Solana's enemies breached the house? Heart pumping wildly, she put the laptop on the bed and prepared to hide underneath it if gunfire erupted. When she heard movement in the hallway, she lowered herself to the floor and scooted under the bed. As someone walked into the room, she tried to quiet her breathing.

"Irena?"

Dumbfounded, Irena replied, "Gordon?"

Before she knew what was happening, he was kneeling at the side of the bed and helping to pull her out. At the feel of his arms around her, Irena experienced as much joy as she did relief. "What are you doing here?"

"Of course, I would come for you," he said.

"I found out what this is all about. Solana is my mother."

Gordon looked stunned at the news, then gunshots erupted. "We've got to go."

Irena grabbed the laptop and took his hand. "I know a way out of here."

They ran to the end of the hallway, where a doorway took them downstairs.

"There's a saferoom somewhere down here," said Irena, when they entered the spa room.

They began moving their hands across the walls, checking for hidden doors. When Irena opened the wooden doors to the sauna, she spotted a section of cedar wall that looked different from the others. Walking up to it, she tapped on the wall. It sounded hollow. She pressed until a door swung open.

Just then, someone burst through the sauna door behind them. Irena swung around to see Solana, grasping her side, blood seeping from a wound in her abdomen. "Help me," she said.

It sounded like footsteps thundering down the stairs into the basement. Irena reached out and pulled Solana with them into the saferoom, shutting the door behind them.

Solana slid down the wall in the small space, lit by a lightbulb hanging from the ceiling. In the center of the room was a lone chair. Irena realized this must also be an interrogation room. She shuddered at what might have occurred here.

Gordon looked from Irena to Solana, questions in his eyes.

"The only reason I brought her in here with us," Irena whispered, "was so she wouldn't expose us. If the people out there are her enemies, they'll kill us all."

"I'm still processing the part about her being your mother."

"Me, too. Believe me. From what I can tell, my father didn't want me to live this life. I think she has been blackmailing him to do her bidding in exchange for me being kept from this."

"You speak as if I'm not here," Solana said, groaning. "I need medical attention."

"Keep your voice down." Irena looked around the room and spotted a towel, which she grabbed and pressed into her mother's abdomen. "Do you have a communication system in here?"

"This room is soundproof," Solana said with a smirk and pointed to a desk. Gordon went over and pulled open a drawer, exposing a computer system that was already powered up. "It's a whole surveillance system," he said. "Several people are moving through the living room. It looks like FBI."

"Sammy must have gotten ahold of Tony," said Irena.

"That stupid little rag doll," Solana said, coughing.

"So, we can go out there?" asked Irena.

"They could mistake us for the enemy," said Gordon. "If there's an intercom, we can introduce ourselves." He looked at Solana, who was apparently not going to give him that information. "I'll just go out there then," he said.

"No, I will."

Before Gordon could protest, Irena had left the saferoom. Taking a deep breath, she slowly made her way out of the sauna, hands raised. She cried out, "I am Irena Martin. I know Special Agent Tony Molinaro. Don't shoot."

"Freeze, FBI," shouted an agent.

"Are you alone?" asked another.

"Solana Petrauskas is hiding in the room behind me. She has lost a lot of blood. The man with her is with me. Agent Molinaro knows him." Irena backed toward the saferoom entrance as the agents descended. They went in to find Solana unconscious and called the paramedics.

After briefly speaking with Gordon, an agent let him come to Irena. He immediately wrapped her in his arms. They stayed that way for a time, Irena not wanting to let go. Because if she did, their time together would be over, and that was something that Irena felt certain she just couldn't face.

30

When an FBI agent cleared his throat, Gordon pulled apart from Irena.

"We're going to need to question you both," he told them.

"Of course," said Gordon.

They followed the agent to the living room, and both gave their accounts separately of the last several hours. When they finished, the head agent told them, "I've got the green light from Special Agent Molinaro to let you go. But it seems there's one pending item for you, Mr. Bradshaw."

Gordon's body tensed. He was afraid of this. He waited for them to slap handcuffs on him to take him in. But his biggest worry was leaving Irena alone after all of this.

"It appears you were wanted in relation to the death of a former business associate." Gordon held his breath as the agent stopped and studied him over the top of his glasses. "It turns out the man's death was determined to have been a suicide, so you're off the hook."

Gordon exhaled a quiet breath. Irena reached over and squeezed his hand.

"There is the matter of some transactions with the deceased that you'll have to clear up with the SEC."

"I will do that first thing tomorrow." Relief flooded through Gordon. "So, we're free to go?"

The agent put his notebook back in his pocket. "Yes, you can go. One of our agents can drop you off somewhere, if needed."

"How about the airport, so we can catch a flight to Vegas. There's someone in the hospital I'd like to see," said Irena.

On the way to the airport, Irena was silent. Gordon tried to make idle conversation, but she barely spoke. Maybe it was the news of Solana being her mother that was keeping her quiet. Probably best to give her space.

At Tucson International Airport, they barely made it onto a red-eye headed for Vegas. When they boarded, the plane was packed, so they had to sit in separate seats. During the flight, Gordon couldn't shake a gnawing feeling he had in his chest. Had all of this been a distraction to Irena? Had Gordon just happened to have been available to help maneuver the mess that had entrapped her?

After de-boarding an hour later and heading to catch a cab to the hospital, Gordon reached for Irena's hand, but she didn't take his. Irritation overtaking him, he stopped walking.

Irena turned toward him. She felt as if there had been more between them, but maybe it was her own wishful thinking. She waited for him to speak. When Gordon didn't say anything, Irena said, "I'm sorry, I know money won't make up for all that happened. But I don't know what else I can offer you."

Gordon stepped closer. She looked up at him.

"I love you, Irena. You may not feel that way about me, but I can't let you leave without telling you. I love you."

Her eyes grew wide, and she said, "You love me?"

Gordon laughed. "Yes, Irena. Why wouldn't I? From the very beginning."

Irena felt her heart fill to overflowing at Gordon's words. But the lump in her throat made it hard to speak. Finally, she found her voice. "I love you, too, Gordon," she said, laughing and crying at the same time.

He smiled and pulled her to him. "Would you want to come home with me to Aspen? See if it's somewhere you'd like to settle?"

"I would love to go to your home," said Irena.

"If you like, it can be your home, too," he said.

"I'm pretty sure I'm already home." Irena melted into Gordon's embrace.

In the hospital a few minutes later, they talked the nurse into letting them in to see Irena's father, even though it was well past visiting hours. "He's doing well," said the woman as she led them down the hushed hall. Irena and Gordon followed, hand-in-hand. If this was a dream, Irena thought, she wanted to stay asleep forever.

They stopped where a guard was still posted. After Gordon told him who they were, he let them pass. As they approached her father's bed, Walter opened his eyes and said, "Irena."

"How are you doing, Dad?" Irena touched his shoulder.

He put his hand out and patted her hand. "Better now that I see you survived Solana."

Irena took a deep breath. "You mean my mother."

Her father looked surprised. He pressed his lips together.

"I'm not upset with you, Dad. I can see why you hid her identity from me."

"I'm so sorry about everything." Her father's eyes were misty.

"I remember the night of the fire," continued Irena.

He gasped. "Solana did terrible things that night. But it's important you know that none of it was your fault. You were just a little thing. She killed a man, then had you set a fire to cover up the evidence. She blamed you by telling the fire marshal you were playing with a lighter. They did an evaluation on you, but I had the record redacted."

Her father paused and swallowed. "Can I get some water?"

Irena put his water glass to his mouth, and he sipped from a straw. When he finished, he resumed. "I made sure nothing like that ever happened again by threatening to expose her if she tried to get you to do anything. We made a deal. She would never tell you the truth of who she was. In return, I did jobs for her throughout the years. But I'd do anything to keep you safe."

"So, that's why you would disappear sometimes?"

"I hope you can forgive me. The reason I didn't always take my medicine was the work. When I wasn't as aware of what I was doing, it was easier." Her father started crying softly.

"Oh, Dad," said Irena, leaning down to gingerly embrace him. "I'm so sorry, too. If only I understood."

Her father looked up and took her face in his hands. "Don't you ever be sorry. I'd do it all again without hesitation. I love you, Irena. Many people love you."

Irena took Gordon's hand and squeezed it, glancing his way and smiling. "I'm beginning to see that."

EPILOGUE

Irena and Gordon's stories are complete, but Hermann's is just beginning...

Hermann was closing the register of the coffee shop for the night when a young girl in a black hoodie came rushing in and went straight for the counter.

"Sorry, hon, but we're closed. I just turned off the espresso machine."

She looked up at him with vivid green eyes, and he saw red hair under her hood.

"Are you Hermann?" She spoke with a fast, southern twang.

"Who's asking?"

"Jimmy sent me. He said I can trust you."

"I guess Jimmy didn't get the memo, but I'm out of the business. Too many gray hairs."

The girl glanced around the shop, then back out to the street. "I was really hoping you could help me. I need to sell and disappear."

Alarm bells rang in Hermann's head. All he could think about was how to get this girl out of the shop before the trouble following her arrived.

"Look, I can refer you to someone, if you want." He pulled a notepad out from under the counter and reached for a pen. "Give me an idea of the merchandise, and I can give you a few names."

"Jimmy told me to trust only you." Her voice was pleading now. "It'll be a big payday for you."

"Hon, nowadays I get my adrenaline rush with a good cup of espresso."

He heard a buzzing sound then, and the girl checked the cellphone in her pocket. The urgency on her face turned to terror. She whipped a small black bag out of her pocket and pushed it into his hands. "Is there an exit in back?"

"Yes," Hermann answered, stunned as she ran toward the back of the shop. He heard the bell on the alley door clang as he opened the bag, gasping when he saw the contents. Hermann knew his gems. He could tell just by looking that these were real diamonds.

Find out what happens to Hermann in *Discovered Deception*...

A NOTE FOR YOU

Dear Reading Gem,

Thanks for spending time with me, Irena and Gordon! While each of the books in the Discovered Truth Series can be read as a standalone, it's fun to experience the progression and get to know the characters. The series progresses as minor characters introduced in each book become main characters in subsequent books. It's exciting to see what they'll do next!

The Discovered Truth series features complex, gutsy women and equally complicated, charismatic men who find themselves immersed in dangerous and intriguing modern-day challenges, such as human trafficking, drug smuggling, national security threats, and identity theft. When the heroine and hero meet, worlds collide and sparks fly, kindling unforgettable romance and intrigue.

If you like the series, please leave a review on any book review platform. Your opinion matters and is incredibly powerful.

Amazon

GoodReads

BookBub

Thanks again and talk soon!

Julie

STAY ENLIGHTENED

Thanks for reading! Let's stay in touch. In appreciation of you, I post updates, insider information, and sneak peeks of upcoming books on my website at https://www.juliebawdendavis.com/fiction. You can also email me at Julie@JulieBawdenDavis.com, follow me on Facebook, and find me on Amazon.

Even better, you can join my VIP Reading Gems mailing list here. I also created a Facebook group especially for you! Join Julie's Reading Gems to get the inside scoop on what's going on with the Discovered Truth Series. Find out how characters are created, and what they might do next. I also ask for Reading Gem opinions on upcoming covers and even plot twists. And there are contests and giveaways!

Escape to Unforgettable Romance and Intrigue...

BOOKS IN THE DISCOVERED TRUTH SERIES

Discovered Beginnings:
(FREE at https://www.juliebawdendavis.com/fiction)
Discovered Secrets
Discovered Memories
Discovered Indiscretions
Discovered Liaisons
Discovered Betrayal
Discovered Denial
Discovered Distractions
Discovered Deception
Discovered Lies
Discovered Vengeance
Discovered Redemption
Discovered Obsession
Discovered Transgressions
Discovered Suspicion
Discovered Escape
Discovered Promises
Discovered Cover-up
Discovered Intentions

Box Sets
The Discovered Truth Series Box Set Books 1-4
The Discovered Truth Series Box Set Books 5-8
The Discovered Truth Series Box Set Books 9-12
The Discovered Truth Series Box Set Books 13-16